I am writing this very small so that no one can read it . . .

Actually that's stupid, because how will I
read it when I'm old and mouldy and want
to know what I was thinking when I was
nearly a teenager? I shall write in code,
so that only I will understand my secret
confession . . .

Read on to find out Alistair's most
embarrassing secret and discover why all
the most loathed people in history have had
a sofa in their bedrooms . . .

Another hilarious instalment of the
War Diaries of Alistair Fury from
award-winning writer, Jamie Rix.

www.kidsatrandomhouse.co.uk

THE WAR DIARIES OF ALISTAIR FURY

The Kiss of Death

Illustrated by Nigel Baines

Jamie Rix

CORGI YEARLING BOOKS

For Louisa
(Mel made flesh)

This edition produced for
The Book People Ltd, Hall Wood Avenue
Haydock, St. Helens, WA11 9UL

THE WAR DIARIES OF ALISTAIR FURY: KISS OF DEATH
A CORGI YEARLING BOOK : 0 440 865557

Published in Great Britain by Corgi Yearling Books,
an imprint of Random House Children's Books

This edition published 2002

3 5 7 9 10 8 6 4 2

Set in 12/14.5pt Comic Sans by Falcon Oast Graphic Art Ltd.

Papers used by Random House Children's Books are natural,
recyclable products made from wood grown in sustainable
forests. The manufacturing processes conform to the
environmental regulations of the country of origin.

Corgi Yearling Books are published by
Random House Children's Books,
61-63 Uxbridge Road, London W5 5SA,
a division of The Random House Group Ltd,
in Australia by Random House Australia (Pty) Ltd,
20 Alfred Street, Milsons Point, Sydney, NSW 2061, Australia,
in New Zealand by Random House New Zealand Ltd,
18 Poland Road, Glenfield, Auckland 10, New Zealand
and in South Africa by Random House (Pty) Ltd, Endulini, 5a
Jubilee Road, Parktown 2193, South Africa

THE RANDOM HOUSE GROUP Limited Reg. No. 954009

A CIP catalogue record for this book is available from the
British Library.

Printed and bound in Great Britain by
Bookmarque Ltd, Croydon, Surrey.

Daily Diary

This diary belongs to Alistair Fury

Age 11

Address 47 Atrocity Road,
Tooting, England

Star Sign Only once, when I waved at Hugh
Grant and he waved back. Or he might have
been hailing a cab - hard to tell. Or it
might not have been Hugh Grant. It was
definitely a cab, though.

Wife's Name Give me a chance. I haven't
even had a kiss yet.

Children's Names I do not want children ever.
I would be too embarrassed to talk to my
children about the birds and the beans
stuff which is frankly silly and actually
not something I know anything about,
except for what Ralph's told me. But as
it's not possible for a human being to turn
inside out like a rubber glove and grow fur
in shady places, I do not believe him.

Notes

Actually that's stupid, because how will I read it when I'm old and mouldy, and want to know what I was thinking when I was nearly a teenager? I shall write in code so that only I will understand my secret confession:

Q: Who is my favourite *lumpy-bumpy thing with a giggle gob* in the world?

A: I only know six and it's definitely not my big sotter-botter, Melodramaticus. It's not my mumble-bumble or Grinny Codface neither, because both of them only exist to stop me having fun. Nor is it Miss Tweetie-Tweet-Tweet (the teacher from Hell) or Mrs Muckly (Piano Warte Taught Here). So it's between Pamela Whitby and Pamela Whitby, but Pamela Whitby hates

This is a brilliant code. Better than the Germans in WW2. It is three days after I wrote it and even I don't know who all these people are! I know they're Mum, Granny, Mrs Muttley, Mel and Miss Bird but IN WHAT ORDER?!

my clothes, so I don't know.

I know what SusSEX is, but I'm still too young and innocent to have been there and

6

---

got the T-shirt. I'm old enough to quiss now too, but I am worried. What do I do if I can taste what she's had for lunch and don't like it?

My last two diaries were confiscated on account of them being too rude about certain people who then found them and beat me up. By the way, if God wants some advice on how to build little brothers in future, I think he should build them with armour-plated shells instead of skin, to withstand all the terrible blows what I get chucked at me from everyone. ➡

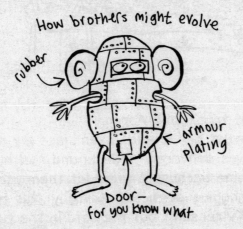

How brothers might evolve

rubber

armour plating

Door— for you know what

And rubber ears too, so the verbal shout-ings just bounce off.

SUNDAY

Here is a list of most-hated people in history:

Genghis Khan
Jack the Ripper
Adolf Hitler
Alistair Fury

What do they all have in common? They all had sofas in their bedrooms.

'Is it true?' said Aaron.

'It must be,' I said. 'Ever since my new sofa was delivered, William and Mel have hated me because I won't let them use it for snogging sessions.' Actually this was the only reason I got the sofa in the first place – to annoy my big brother and sister. And also because Ralph had said it was time us Revengers got into kissing.

Not each other, of course. I checked with Ralph and he didn't mean in that way at all.

Ralph has changed. His body is sprouting hairs like the way blotting-paper sprouts watercress in Reception Class. And he uses a deodorant now at weekends. We were meeting in our secret bus shelter by the McDrive-In, because Ralph had brought along a Shower Catalogue and didn't want anyone seeing us looking at it.

'What's so naughty about showers?' I asked. He turned the page to a picture of a naked woman behind a shower curtain. You could see her ankles and shower cap.

SHOWER MONTHLY

Boiling hot or freezing cold... is there an In between?

Unblocking hair

PLUS

WHAT KYLIE WEARS IN THE SHOWER

I tried to look at the bath mat and pretend I wasn't interested, but my eyes kept drifting upwards. My mouth went dry and my heart beat so loudly that everyone in the street could hear it. I had to think of the most boring thing in the universe to stop the noise. I thought of French vocab:

Le can-can is a bird called a 'twocan'.

Mon père a un moustache is 'my pear has a moustache'.

Le chat is 'the chat' as in the common phrase, *Un telephone chat-line*.

We Revengers have a secret code to stop us talking if a stranger stands next to us and waits for a bus. The secret code is 'Shhhhh'. Sometimes buses pull in to pick us up and drivers get angry when we don't get on. A bus stopped today and the driver was a psychopath. He had scary sideburns growing out of his mouth. So we got on and held the rest of our meeting at the back of the bus in little fairy whispers.

I wanted to know how Ralph thought we were going to get a kiss when none of us knew any girls who weren't our sisters or cousins.

'Girls prefer to kiss people they don't know,' he said, 'because they don't know enough about you to hate you yet.'

'Yeah, but if you don't know them,' I said, 'how can you ask for a kiss?'

'You don't ask,' said Ralph, 'you trick them. You pretend you're dying and need the kiss of life. Or switch the lights off at a party and steal a kiss in the dark. Or tell her you're a spy like James Bond and have to pass her a secret message mouth to mouth!'

The party sounded most practical. Trouble was, none of us had ever thrown one before. We weren't exactly sure what to do. We knew we had to move all the furniture against the walls and put newspaper on the floor, but we didn't know why.

'Do people bring their pets to parties?' asked Aaron.

'Maybe the newspaper's there to give you something to read while you're kissing,' said Ralph.

'When it gets boring, you mean? Because I have heard,' I said, 'that some kisses can go on for so long that worried parents report their children as missing.'

Aaron and Ralph wanted to have the kissing party as soon as possible. 'Next Sunday, your place,' they said.

'Can't,' I said. 'Next Sunday is Mum's new cookbook launch.'

'Saturday then,' said Ralph.

'Mrs Muttley's piano concert,' I said.

They accused me of making excuses because I was scared of kissing, but I really am that busy next weekend.

'Then when can we come?' said a disappointed Ralph.

'In about five years,' I said. 'When Mum isn't precious about her new kitchen any more.'

Mum's just had a new kitchen fitted for her TV show. The lights are so bright that it makes us all sweat like heavyweight boxers, which is nice in the food. 'Mmmm! What's on the Sweat Trolley tonight, Mum?'

Walked five miles home after bus conductor threw us off the bus for not having any money to pay our fares. The three of us are now outlaws, which is good because girls love bad boys.

At home my big brother and sister were waiting for me. Both wanted to borrow my sofa tonight as they'd got hot-totty lined up. But when I said no, they said, 'Right, you tightwad, you're dead!' Which was a nice thing to say on the holiest day of the week.

Mel's current boyfriend is called Roger. She never stops telling us how beautiful he

Ho-ho! Bring me a dry pair of pants!

is, but he's got spots like a Chelsea Bun and nasty cheap trainers, which is why I secretly call him Roger the Todger. He gave Mel a bracelet made from hairs that grow on top of an elephant's head and she thinks it's a sign of endless love. It's a sign of endless bald elephants, stupid!

As if I didn't suffer enough in the first diary!

WIGS R US XXL

WIG GLUE

William thinks he's a babe magnet because he says he's got more girlfriends than all of Westlife put together. He's not a magnet. He's flypaper and it's all the dirty flies what nobody else wants who stick to him! The present girlfriend is a bad-tempered bluebottle called Rosie.

HORROR!

Granny Constance blew in for Sunday supper like a cold arctic wind. She doesn't like me. In fact there's not much she does like, except nattering on about her aches and pains, and her Scrabble Club, which she thinks is the centre of the universe. Like we should all care deeply that Elsie made 'carbuncle' last week on a triple-word score using a 'car' that was already down there!

'Not a real car, you understand, just the word,' she kept saying.

'Yes, Granny! For the fifty millionth time, I'd worked that out for myself!'

We don't eat Sunday lunch in the Fury household. That would be too normal. Because my mum is a TV chef we have to eat at supper, and never beef or lamb, always disgusting food like sturgeon and chicken livers and raw goat in gravy. Today it is pheasant. Yuck!

ONE OF LIFE'S LITTLE PROBLEMS

Tomorrow I have a French test with Miss Bird. She calls it her *Grand Examination de French*. Here is an actual conversation I once had with a French teacher:

15

'J'ai numque been any bonbon a French.'

'Paraquat?'

'Because I can't see the point of it. Everyone speaks English where I live.'

This conversation neatly sums up why I hate French and am not completely fluent yet. I desperately need a lovely person to test me on vocab before supper.

Could I find a lovely person to help me? William and Mel would rather I died than got a proper education, Mum's too busy phoning round for a duck-billed platypus – not to eat, just to put on display at her book launch next week – and Dad's too busy

who said I couldn't draw a platy...thing?

tiling. He's gone DIY mad. It's pathetic. It's taken him a whole week to stick up one tiny square of tiles behind the sink in the new kitchen! I think DIY must stand for 'Dad Is Yelling!' because every time he cuts

← even thugs are shocked

keep out

himself he swears really loudly. It's brilliant! When he's shouting **s*i*g*t** and **p*ck**q**m*s** and **f***yw**g*e** I can swear as much as I like and nobody can hear me!

Mum's launch party's got an Australian Beach Barbecue theme because her new book is called *Playing with Fire – Cooking in the Great Outdoors*. She says that if this book doesn't sell well, we'll have to live in a rented caravan and eat fish skins and pig trotters for the rest of our lives. That's

why it's so important that this party's a success. Everyone who I've never heard of is coming and a man called Cornelius is helping to organize it. He's an inferior designer, which probably means he's cheap.

Anyway, it turned out that the only person who was free to help me with my French homework was Granny. So I said in my loudest most sarcastic voice, 'Oh thank you, Granny. At least one of my family loves me. I wish you lived here all the time instead of my real family.'

But Granny was just as selfish as the rest.

'Ask me words in French first,' I said.

'Cowpat,' she said. 'That's another good one. Thirty-six on a triple-word score.' Her mind is Scrabbled.

While Dad was carving the pheasant there was an unsavoury incident. Mr E, our pug dog, jumped on a chair and shoved his ugly mug into the puddle of blood that was lapping round the bird like a moat. Then he started drinking. I think Mr E is a Vampire Dog. If I was to hit him with a

18

cricket bat he'd explode with blood like a mosquito. Dad only noticed when the pheasant started moving, floating slowly across the meat plate towards the dog's sucking mouth. Mr E caught a flick with an oven glove right up his bum, which made him squeal and run off into the garden.

Granny said, 'That dog's disgusting. And that clumsy cat's no better.'

Our cat, Napoleon, had his tail chopped off in a cat flap, which means he's always falling over. When the builders were here rebuilding the back of the house they had to wear hard hats all the time because Napoleon kept plunging off the scaffolding.

mmm...be raining cats and dogs before long

Granny gave me a book called *How to Hypnotize Your Pet into Better Behaviour* and said it was my job to cure our pets.

19

an ex pheasant

'Why me?' I said.

'Because your brain is the most beastly in the family,' said Granny.

Don't think calling me an animal is particularly funny. Do I go to the loo in the park where everyone can see me? No. Not for a long time now.

The pheasant was full of bullets. Granny choked on one and coughed her potatoes onto my plate. I was told not to make a fuss.

see, I'm telling the TOOTH!!

'But there's two teeth in my peas,' I said.

'Don't be so stupid,' said Granny, taking her dentures back off my plate, 'there's no *t* in *peas*.'

That was when William asked me how my French was coming on at school. For obvious reasons,* this was not a conversation I wanted to have in front of Mum and Dad. I said, 'OK. But if you really want to know, I think the language sounds cissy.'

* i.e. me and French get on like stomachs and salmonella

'Is that why you came bottom of the year last term?' he said.

'Did you?' said Mum.

'Oh, sorry,' said William. 'I forgot. Alice lost last term's report so none of us know how he did.' William was up to something. He was smirking like a jackal. 'Oh!' he gasped suddenly. 'Look what I found.' And he stood up and produced my report from under his seat.

'Where did you get that?' asked Dad.

'Under Alice's mattress,' said William. Then he leaned across the table and whispered in my ear, 'Sofa so good, Alice. What do you think?' This was his payback for my sofa refusal.

The report was a stinker. I was bottom of everything and Mum and Dad sent me to my room. As I was leaving the kitchen, I witnessed William and Mel shaking slippery, treacherous hands.

I was lying on my bed trying to think up a revenge when I saw Granny's book and had an idea that would for ever put an end to Mel and William torturing me mentally. Hypnotism! I could bring them under my power and use them as zombie slaves! First, though, I practised on Mr E and Napoleon, in case I got the technique wrong and blew up their brains *by accident.*

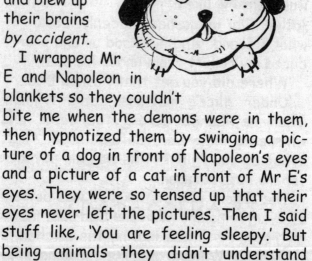

exploding dog brain

I wrapped Mr E and Napoleon in blankets so they couldn't bite me when the demons were in them, then hypnotized them by swinging a picture of a dog in front of Napoleon's eyes and a picture of a cat in front of Mr E's eyes. They were so tensed up that their eyes never left the pictures. Then I said stuff like, 'You are feeling sleepy.' But being animals they didn't understand English, so I changed what I was saying to:

'Who's a good boy, then? Go to sleep for Daddy-waddy!' And when they still looked blank I woofed and miaowed until their eyes closed.

21.05 – Napoleon just woke up, leaped at the door and scratched to be let out. At the same time Mr E shot halfway up the curtains, slipped off, did a back flip and cut his ear. Napoleon is licking it better even as I write. What have I done? Am I the creator of the first four-legged, blood-sucking monster? Perhaps I should change my name to Dr Frankenstein! Don't think I'm quite ready to hypnotize humans yet.

FRANKENCAT

21.45 – Went downstairs to say sorry, but Mum didn't believe me when I promised her that I didn't know how my report had got under my mattress. 'It wasn't me,' I said. 'I mean, how was I to know Miss Bird had given me the worst report I've ever had? I'm not a mind reader, am I? I can't read words through brown envelopes even if the flap had mysteriously come unstuck *by accident*!'

TILED BY
MR FURY
NO SPLASHING

Dad was taking no part in this discussion. He'd just finished his tiling. From the fuss he was making you'd have thought he'd just finished tiling St Paul's Cathedral or the gents' loo at Euston Station. He was running in and out of the kitchen admiring his handiwork.

'Why?' I asked.

'It's an old DIY trick,' he said. 'I run into

the hall and make myself forget that I've just finished the tiling, then I run back into the kitchen as quick as I can to see what I think of my work before I remember it was me who did it.'

Have checked 'insanity' on Encarta. It does not skip a generation. I am very afraid.

22.05 – Have just thought of brilliant back-up revenge plan. William and Mel have gone out with Rosie and Roger. As they say in the fairy tales, '*While the brats are away the nice will play!*'

22.30 – Mum and Dad have gone to bed.

22.34 – Crept into William and Mel's bedrooms and stole their precious address books. Then climbed out of William's window onto the half-roof over the kitchen. Unfortunately I had timed my revenge to coincide with a light shower. I was soaked in a second. It was windy too, so I got down on all fours and slid across the slates. Then, when I reached the edge of the roof, I hid their address books in the guttering. If they were going to ruin my life I was going to ruin theirs! I had made sure that they would lose touch with all their friends!

But as I was crawling back to the window I put my knee on a dodgy slate. I heard it crack under my weight. I remember thinking, why's there never a big black hole to swallow you up when you want one? Next thing I knew, there was. My right leg was stuck through the kitchen ceiling, which, considering how much money Mum and Dad had just paid to have it done up, was about the worst thing that I could possibly have done. Worse even than farting in a lift with Britney Spears. If Mum and Dad ever knew that I was responsible for making this hole, they would sell me off to an orphanage and burn my birth certificate.

I wrenched my leg out of the hole and slid across the slates to the sycamore tree that overhung the roof. Then I broke off the biggest branch I could handle and placed it carefully next to the hole. Satisfied that Mum and Dad would think that the branch was to blame for the damage, I turned to go back to bed, only to discover that I was not alone. Standing at the window, watching my every move with evil eyes and nasty little smiles on their faces, were William and Mel. I was fried frog on toast!

'Or you will be,' said Will, 'if you don't get our address books back!'

But in rescuing the address books I fell through the same hole again and made it *twice* as big! And this time I got stuck up to my waist. I looked like some freaky mushroom creature that grew out of roofs! 'Help!' I said. 'Help me out!'

'Can't,' said Mel. 'But I'm sure that hungry rat we just saw diving down the hole can.'

I was out of that roof in a flash. It was like unplugging a bath. The rain gushed down through the hole onto Mum's new floor, and by the time I'd climbed back through the window, the kitchen was sloshing with water.

'What am I going to do?' I pined to my brother and sister.

'Suffer,' they said. And suffer I did.

I couldn't get to sleep. I was praying for

a miracle, praying that the hole in the roof would scab over and heal. When I did finally nod off I had a highly symbolic dream.

MY HIGHLY SYMBOLIC DREAM, THAT I HAD

I am sitting in a kennel with a chain around my neck. There is something sniffing my bum, which means that I must be a dog, and the sniffing is another dog doing what comes natural. Only this other dog is not natural. Oh no. It's a cat! It's Napoleon, with a lead in his mouth!

Woke up to find that I was wearing a dog collar and lead, which my big brother and sister were holding. 'You're a very bad boy!' they whispered. 'And unless you want Mum to know the truth about the roof, you will be our slave for ever. And when either of us wants to use your sofa, we will!'

And if I didn't do as I was told? Exposure, humiliation, punishment, shame, exile, loneliness, insanity and suckling by wolves!

Hmm . . . tough choice.

MONGDAY

05.45 – Oh joy! Have just discovered that last night's light shower was in fact a hurricane, and our garden is full of fallen trees! Oh thank you, Hermione. I love you.

They've already given the hurricane a name.

The garden looks like a jungle and Mum and Dad think that the tree caused the hole in the roof. I'm free! Unless William and Mel choose to tell the truth, of course.

It is quite spooky that I was praying for a miracle last night and this morning I got one. Some people might think that makes me like God or something, commanding the forces of Nature where King Canute failed. But I don't know – *Almighty Alistair, Alistair the God, Muhammad Alistair* – none of them sounds quite right somehow. Being God would definitely be handy, though. I could put plagues of frogs in Mel's bed.

05.48 – Another extraordinary thing – there are people up at this time of the morning! In cars, on bikes, walking. I *never* knew! I thought everyone stayed asleep till I woke up.

Mum is crying. Because of the ruination of her beautiful new kitchen and the distinct lack of garden, she now thinks her launch party is going to be pants, and if her launch party is pants she won't sell any copies of her new book, and if she doesn't sell any copies of her new book, she'll be banged up in a debtor's prison. I've got news for her. With recipes like Exotic Bananas and Offal Tofu, Cobra Kebabs and Porcupine Patties she won't sell any copies of her new book anyway!

She phoned her party organizer,

Cornelius, to tell him about the disaster and started him crying too. I could hear him blubbing down the phone from the other side of the room. In between sobs they both agreed that what was needed was a quick local builder to patch the roof and re-lay the floor. But when Mum asked Dad to sort it out he ignored her and carried on stroking his tiles.

'What a professional job,' he said proudly. 'Not even a hurricane can knock them off.' Then he told Mum that no builder was necessary as he would put his expert DIY skills to good use and mend the roof himself. Mum looked depressed.

06.15 – Heard barking from the sky. Thought it might be raining cats and dogs, but it was in fact Mr E stuck in the sycamore tree over the kitchen roof. The fireman who came to rescue him had been clearing up after the hurricane since three o'clock in the morning, and a stupid tree-climbing dog that thought it was a cat was just what he *didn't* need right now!

I remember thinking '. . .a dog that thought it was a cat . . .' and putting two and two together. Maybe I *have* got hypnotic powers after all! *

On the way down the ladder Mr E jumped off the fireman's shoulder. Obviously, thinking he was a cat, he was expecting to land on his feet. He landed on a brick and Mum had to rush him to the Blue Cross Hospital.

'Aren't you even a tiny bit concerned about your dog?' I said to Dad, who by now had crawled into the kitchen sink and was kissing his tiles *with his eyes closed*! *

'Little beauties,' he said. 'Masterful grouting.'

06.55 – While Mum was away, a taxi pulled up and Granny Constance appeared at the front door. She got Dad to pay the taxi and me to carry her three suitcases in. 'Put them in the spare room,' she said. 'I'm staying till my house is fixed.'

'Oh no!' I said. 'That could be for ever. How badly's it broken?'

'It's the chimney,' she said. 'And I thought you said you wanted me to live here, Alistair.'

Oh heck. I think I did say that, didn't I?

Dad was panicking. 'Mum, I really ought to check with Celia first,' he said, sitting on the suitcases so I couldn't take them upstairs.

'Nonsense,' she said. 'Who wears the trousers in this house?'

← DAD'S Trousers

Obviously Granny, because five minutes later Dad had organized a builder to mend her roof and she was making herself comfortable in the sitting room.

'Are you expecting to be pampered?' I asked nervously, in case she was thinking that I might be her personal slave.

'Don't be ridiculous,' she said. 'When you've done the suitcases, I'll have a cup of tea, milk, three sugars, and a packet of chocolate biscuits.'

Ode to Joy

Oh joy!
Granny's come to stay.
I wonder if she knows when
She's going to go away?
(yet)

The builder, Mr Stratford, must be charging Dad a lot, because Dad's face was as white as a sheet when he came off the phone. But, as I said to Dad, no price is too much to pay to get Granny home again *fast*. He understood.

07.59 – Mum brought Mr E back from the dog hospital. His front leg is in plaster. Mum said he was lucky not to break his little neck as well. Not lucky for us, obviously.

Mum seemed surprised to hear that Granny was staying, and even more surprised to hear that Dad had managed to phone a builder to mend the hole in Granny's roof but not the one in ours!

'I told you,' said Dad. '*I'm fixing ours.*'

From the look on Mum's face I think we're in for a bumpy ride.

William and Mel are furious that Granny is living with us. They pinched my arm and pushed me into the airing cupboard.

'She hates fun,' said Mel. 'She'll stop me seeing Roger.'

'And me seeing Rosie,' said William. 'It'll just be Scrabble, Scrabble, Scrabble!'

'And horse-racing,' I said. 'She likes that too.'

'Oh shut up!' said Mel. 'It's all your fault for saying you wanted her to live with us.'

'I didn't mean it,' I said.

'Well it's a bit late to say sorry now!' said Mel.

'Virgin!' said William.

'I'm not!' I said.

'You don't even know what a virgin is,' laughed Mel.

'I do!'

'What is it then?'

'Not telling,' I said cleverly.

Actually I don't have a clue what a virgin is, so I asked the Revengers at school.

'Isn't it someone who works in a church?' said Aaron. 'You know, collects money and washes the white dresses.'

'Can't be,' said Ralph, 'because it's a rude word. Richard Branson's one, I think.'

'So it's another word for men with beards?'

'No,' said Aaron, 'because women can be virgins too.'

'Is it *women* with beards then?' I said.

But Aaron said it couldn't be, because who'd ever seen a picture of the Virgin Mary with a beard. None of us had.

We were having a secret meeting in the teachers' loos to discuss which girls we should invite to our party. We used to meet in the Second Year loos, but mothers complained that the bubby little Second Years were coming home with wet trousers from lack of access to facilities. So we moved to the First Year loos, where a similar epidemic of dampness occurred. Hopefully the teachers will have better bladder control.

They certainly have much nicer loo paper than we have. If you blow your nose on their paper it absorbs stuff, but on our

paper, stuff just slides around like eggs in a greasy pan.

Back to girls.

'I don't know anything about them,' I said, 'except how poisonous older sisters are.'

'Girls like body hair,' said Ralph. But he was only saying that because he's got sixteen hairs under his arms and one on his nipple. He calls it his hairy chest, but I think you need two for that, at least.

'Do they like virgins?' I asked, but nobody knew.

We decided to list the girls we did know, but it was a very short list: three mums, Ralph's sister, Mel, Miss Bird, Aaron's cousin, Mrs Muttley, Granny Constance and Pamela Whitby. We all liked Pamela

The girls we know

erm...

um..

nope

er...

oh dear

Whitby, but sadly since I spilled ketchup on her best blouse at Nathan's Mex Tex No Sex Disco Party last week she hasn't talked to me. I've ruined her reputation apparently. I told her it would wash, but she wouldn't listen.

37

The awfulness of the list, however, meant that we would have to find and meet new girls to ask to our party. We made more lists.

WHERE TO MEET GIRLS
In make-up shops · The ballet
Flower shows · Gymkhanas

WHAT WE ARE LOOKING
FOR IN GIRLS
Not baff · A sense of humour
i.e. must laugh at our jokes
Terrific personality

WHICH GIRLS ARE KNOWN TO
BE THE BEST KISSERS
Girls with big lips like fish

Our list-making was rudely cut short by repeated knocking on loo door, then desperate 'let me in's from Mr Labinjo (Biology).

Aaron put on his best Miss Bird voice and squeaked, 'If I could come out I would, Mr Labinjo, but I'm currified!' We tried to stop ourselves laughing, but a snorty peep squeaked out through my lips. Luckily Aaron was thinking on his feet. 'Whoops!' he said
as Miss Bird.

38

'Stop listening to my farts, Mr Labinjo!'
And we heard him run away.

When we looked back at our lists we realized they were pathetic. We needed help from an expert. So we dragged Panos Papayoti out of the corridor. Panos is our age, but so hairy that if he walked on all fours and grew a pair of floppy ears he could win Cruft's.

'I can't speak to you,' he said when he saw it was me.

'Why not?' I said.

'Because my little brother, Dimitri, is playing in Mrs Muttley's piano concert next to you,' he said. 'And my dad says you're the enemy because you might be better than Dimitri and he wants Dimitri to be the best.'

'Dimitri *is* the best,' I said. 'When I hear him play I feel inadequate, because he's only six and I am pants by comparison.'

'Doesn't matter,' said Panos. 'I wouldn't put it past my dad to have your arms broken.'

Now *that* would hurt.

Ralph told Panos to forget the concert. We wanted to know if he knew any girls. He said he didn't. Did he know what girls liked, then?

'Chocolate,' he said.

'No, that's you,' said Aaron. 'You're the one with pockets full of Mars Bars.'

'Oh yes,' said Panos. 'I forgot.'

Then Ralph asked him if he knew what a virgin was and he said it was someone who hadn't had sex yet. I *knew* I'd heard it before.

'Actually, I *did* know that,' I said.

'You did not,' said the other Revengers.

'I did.'

'Why do you want to know?' asked Panos. 'Are you lot virgins?'

I wanted to say yes, because I was, but something hot-blooded stirred inside and I said, 'No, of course not. Are we, lads?'

'No, of course not,' said Ralph and Aaron.

'Oh,' said Panos, 'because I am.'

The bell rang for the end of break, so we squeezed out of the window and double-backed down the corridor, past Mr Labinjo hopping up and down outside the loo door.

Funny how many teachers were late for their classes after break! Miss Bird had the back of her skirt tucked into the top of her pants, and when she found out she made our test twice as hard because she knew we'd been peeking.

MON GRAND EXAMINATION DE FRENCH
By Alistair Fury

Translate the following words into French:

I love you – Ooh·la·la

I hate you – Gerroutamaface

Where is the toilet? – Vite! Vite! Haute cuisine!

The weekend – Le weekend

The hair salon – Le hair salon

I like yoghurt – Je t'adore le rice pudding

I prefer ice cream – Je preferez una paloma blanca

The train station – Waterloo

I think – You stink

To be sick – Le Ricky Martin

Translate the following words into English:

Le timbre – The Timberland shoes

Après – Ski

Les pantalons – The pongy people next door who hang their pants on the line

Au secours! – Have you got the time on you? No rush.

Kilo – Pound (weight)

La maison – My son
Le nez – The horse
Sourir – There's a mouse in the house
La soeur – Sewer or Melanie (same thing)
Le frère – The deep-fat fryer

1/20

Unfortunately, because of my poor show there will now be a second test tomorrow. I said to Miss Bird, 'But what's the point? I'll never speak French after I leave school.'

And she said, 'Everyone needs French, Fury. It's the language of love.'

NOTE TO MOI-SELF
Must try harder in
French!

Got home to find Mum hugging a strawberry humbug – actually it was a man in stripy pink clothes. It was Cornelius and both of them were crying. The garden was still full of tree and the roof was still full of hole.

Surprise surprise, Dad had *not* managed to fix it. He was sitting with his back against the kitchen table. The floor was covered in blood where he'd smashed his knuckles with a hammer, and Napoleon was lapping away like a bilge pump. But something was wrong. Dad was crying too. His stupid sink tiles had finally fallen off.

Crying is something I shall never do in front of my children. It makes a child think that he's responsible for his father's pain and misery. Which in this case I *am*, of course, but he doesn't need to know that. There are some secrets so secret that nobody should ever know them. Like who you pretend your pillow is when you kiss it.

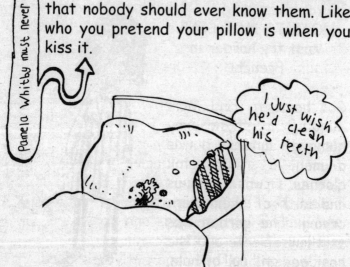

Having failed to mend the hole, as Mum said he would, Dad now phoned the builder, but Mr Stratford couldn't start on our house till he'd finished on Granny's. And he couldn't go any faster, because he had a metal plate in his shoulder that rusted up in the wet weather.

Dad came off the phone and said to Mum, 'I've let you down, Celia.'

'Yes,' she said. 'You have.'

So he said he'd make it up to her with his expert DIY skills. From the broken branches he would build her an authentic bush barbecue for her launch party.

'You don't have to,' said Mum.

'No, I want to,' said Dad. 'It'll be a triumphant centrepiece!'

Mum looked depressed again.

Cornelius is recreating Bondi Beach in our back garden with sand and surfboards. Mum has been trying to book a famous party entertainer called the Living Lightbulb, who juggles with seagulls and swallows electric eels so his insides light up, but apparently he's dead.

R.I.P.
'see...I told you I was ill'

So she's settled on a Rolf Harris tribute band called the Two Rolfs, who are two blokes with beards. One can't paint and the other can't sing. Neither is Australian.

er...can you tell what it is yet?

Cornelius took me outside and explained his vision. 'I see a beach,' he said with a dramatic sweep of his hands, 'and a big rubber shark with horrid old teeth, cans of lager on dunes, cute little crocodiles and

Why trees?... I always fancied a swimming pool

a live koala scampering up a eucalyptus tree.' He stopped, took a peek at the devastated garden and closed his eyes. 'I am strong. I am strong. I *am* strong!' he told himself, until suddenly he wasn't.

While he beat his breast and sobbed, I ran away and went upstairs to learn the language of love.

I was stopped by Granny, who wanted to know why the house was so cold.

'Because there's a hole in the roof!' I said.

'Disgraceful,' she said. 'Where's my tea?'

I never got to my bedroom. After Granny's tea I had to make twelve sandwiches for William and a smoked salmon bagel for Mel. Then it was time for supper. Mum couldn't be bothered to cook, what

47

Not the actual oven, obviously. Some food was cooked in it.

with it raining in the kitchen, so supper was a microwave.

Granny wanted to know when Mum had decided to become a lazy cook, which prompted Mum to suggest that we should all go out for dinner. But Dad said he couldn't afford it, not with the building bills. I did notice that for all her complaining, Granny ate three helpings and drank the best part of a whole bottle of wine.

After supper she complained that she couldn't get comfy on our sofa and didn't like the programmes we watched on our telly. She made Dad and me drive over to her house to fetch her own TV and favourite armchair – only the armchair wouldn't fit in the car, so while Dad drove back with the TV, I pushed the armchair all the way home on my own. It was fine until I got a wheel stuck in a manhole and

caused a traffic jam. That was when a driver told me to get some L-plates and called me a f****y g***t p**-*****n t*t*f*****s p*x**ktu**ct! Luckily I'd heard it all before off Dad.

20.05 – Granny has positioned her TV in front of our TV, but this is OK, because she has positioned her armchair in front of our sofa so we can't see the TV anyway.

20.06 – Went upstairs to learn French, but spent miserable evening on landing instead. Big brother and sister threw me out of my own bedroom so that they could use my sofa. William had Rosie over between eight and nine, while Mel and

*That's because he *never* goes out, because if he does he has to take his embarrassing grandad with him. His grandad shouts at lampposts, apparently.

Roger the Todger took up residence between nine and ten. Meanwhile I was outside doing William's homework, copying out an essay by Piggy Moore, who's the school genius and always gets an A. *

21.25 – After Rosie had gone, William came upstairs and told me to lie on his bed for half an hour, because it needed warming up before he could sleep in it.

'Do it yourself,' I said.

'I don't want to,' he replied. 'And if you don't do it I shall tell Mum and Dad about the hole.'

'That's not fair,' I said. 'I'm not a slave, I'm your little brother.'

'As they say in France, Alice, tough titties! *C'est la vie!*'

'Actually, it's *viande*,' I told him. '*C'est la viande!* Ignoramus!'

50

TUESDAY

06.40 – 'Oh, slave,' said William's voice. 'Wakey-wakey. My socks and pants need warming on the radiator.'

'Mine too,' said Mel. 'And I'd like a cup of tea, please.'

'And me,' said William.

'But I'm asleep,' I said.

'I'm sorry,' said Mel, 'but did our slave just answer back? Maybe we should go and have a word with Mummy and Daddy, William?'

'Good idea,' said Will, 'and then we'll cut his tongue out.'

'I'll get your tea,' I said.

There was a knock on my bedroom wall. 'While you're up, Alistair,' said Granny Constance, 'I'll have a cup too. And a chocolate biscuit.'

We took our shoes and socks off for breakfast and let the rainwater lap around our ankles. Dad had rigged an umbrella under the hole and three buckets on the floor to catch the worst of the drips.

'Is it just me or is it cold in this house?' asked Granny.

51

This time I did not dignify her stupid question with an answer.

Then William gave Mum and Dad a school note that he should have given them last week, and nobody shouted at him. This does not seem fair, because I was SENT TO MY ROOM for forgetting to give them my report. He should at least be publicly humiliated by being made to walk up the street with a cardboard sign round his neck saying, ➡

I THINK OF NOBODY BUT MYSELF — PLEASE FEEL FREE TO PELT ME WITH ROTTEN TOMATOES AND/OR OLD NAPPIES.

William's school note was about his French exchange who's arriving on Wednesday.

Mum suddenly looked worried. 'Oh dear,' she said. 'But where will he sleep?'

'He?' said William. 'It's a *she*. Name's Giselle. And she can sleep in my room.'

'She cannot!' shouted Granny, exploding

in an eye-bulging rant about the younger generation having no manners or morals, and how policemen look so young nowadays, and wasn't it a shame that they couldn't belt cheeky kids around the ear any more. And how in her day lemonade was tuppence ha'penny a bottle, and nobody locked their back doors, and Thursday night was always dripping night!

I asked what dripping was. It's beef fat, apparently. I thought Granny Constance meant bath night, when the whole family dried themselves in front of the fire and dripped all over the carpet.

'If you don't mind!' shouted Mum. 'This is *my* house, Constance, and *I* will make the decisions! Giselle will be sleeping in the spare room, William. You are only fourteen.'

'Nearly fifteen,' he said. 'And anyway, *she's* sixteen!'

'But I'm in the spare room,' said Granny Constance, 'and I'm not moving.'

But if Granny stays William will have to move in with me. 'No!' I said. 'Last time we shared a room, William shaved off my head – I mean, hair. And everything I wanted, he always wanted the opposite. I wanted the window open, he wanted it closed. I wanted the light on, he wanted it off. I wanted to breathe, he wanted to fart like a cow. I'd rather sleep in a tent in the

garden than spend another night with William's wind.'

'Believe me, we'd all be happier if you lived in the garden,' said William, 'but you can't, because there's a dead tree in it.'

don't panic
alistair fury!

So surviving William is going to happen unless Granny leaves soon, and Dad said that Granny can't move back into her own house while her roof's still leaking. I offered to buy her an umbrella but nobody laughed.

Granny Constance noticed that Mr E was not around. She said that pugs were very sensitive and he'd probably run away to escape from all the filthy language that was uttered in our house. I told her that Mr E was always running away and finding him was simple. I'd walk around the house shoving Mum's hand mirror into little nooks and crannies. Then when Mr E saw himself he'd howl with fear, because he'd never seen anything quite as ugly as his own reflection!

Found him up the same tree. The same fireman got him down again too. Unfortunately, while he was still on the ladder, Napoleon launched a savage attack on the fireman's ankles. In trying to protect himself, the fireman let go of Mr E and the dog sprang to the ground with all the grace and agility of a no-tailed cat.

'If we have to come out again for your mad dog,' said the fireman, 'he stays in that tree.'

'He won't be climbing anywhere ever again,' I said. Mr E was not moving.

'If he's dead,' said Dad, sniffing money to pay for the building work, 'You'll be hearing from my solicitor. Or shall we say no more about it, and you can just pump the water out of our kitchen for free?'

'I'll pretend I didn't hear that,' said the fireman.

'Fair enough,' said Dad, backing down in the face of the much more muscly man.

I sat in the back of the car with William on the way to school. A stunned Mr E slept on the seat between us. Mum was taking him back to the Blue Cross Hospital. It's strange how faces soften during sleep, how ugly mugs can suddenly look quite pretty. Not Mr E, though. He was born pug ugly and pug ugly he'll stay till they invent plastic surgery for pooches. If I was him I'd take a nose job!

S,A,C,₃R,E, B,₃L,E,U,R,G,₂H,₄

First lesson, French. F*u*t and v*g*t*b*e*! I forgot to revise.

UN OTHER FRENCH TEST
By Alistair Fury

Translate the following words
into English:

La plume de ma tante – The feathers in the hat of my tarantula

L'oiseau – Hello cheeky!

Crudités – Swear words

Quel âge as-tu? – Which planet are you from?

Bonsoir – No idea. If you mean bonsai that's 'goodnight'

Tête-à-tête – Two French tests back to back

Il y a un flocon de neige sur ma veste – A flock of gypsies have stolen my vet

Peut-être – To be a cat

Mange-tout – Eat all your greens or you won't grow up to be a big boy

Un table – ~~A table~~ ~~A table tennis bat~~ ~~A table~~ ~~A tall story~~ ~~A table~~ A stable

0/10

Tried to explain to Miss Bird that I was a refugee from the hurricane and had no house left in which to do my homework. 'Dad's lost his tiles, the house's lost its roof, Mum's lost her mind and we're flooded. We're living like rude peasants in Victorian England. Have pity on a poor urchin, s'il view plate!' *

She gave me extra homework to do. A worksheet. *Merde!*

I know what that word means.

Revengers met in teachers' loos again. Miss Bird picking on me was top of the agenda. Aaron said I should hypnotize her to make her nicer, but I don't think hypnotism works if you're made out of stone. By way of protest, Ralph blew his nose on a towel with *Headmistress* embroidered in the corner. He said it was a blow against the system!

We decided that William and Mel were to blame for my extra homework, having stolen my sofa and not let me into my bedroom. Aaron had a brilliant idea for payback: 'If they live by fire they must die by fire too!'

'I'm not setting fire to them,' I said. 'There are limits. Anyway, the fire brigade wouldn't put them out, because they're fed up with saving Mr E.'

'No,' said Aaron. 'We destroy the one thing they love the most.'

'Mirrors,' I said.

'No, your sofa.'

'You're not destroying my sofa,' I said.

'All right,' said Aaron, 'we'll just remove a few slats so the bottom collapses and they fall through.'

'Brilliant,' said Ralph. 'And while they're trapped by the cushions we can hypnotize them so they become *our* slaves for ever!'

'That might be dangerous,' I said. 'I've

only done the hypnotism on pets. I don't know if it works on humans.'

'You can try on me,' said Aaron. 'But no funny stuff! I've heard of hypnotists who get people to take off all their clothes and behave like chickens.'

MUST KiSS Alistair

We swore we wouldn't do that, and Ralph promised that if it worked we'd use our powers to hypnotize fit girls into coming to our snogging party.

We got Aaron to sleep by making him concentrate on my moving finger and saying things like, 'Go to sleep, Aaron, go to sleep. You are getting tired and sleepy. Sleepy, sleepy, sleepy. Your eyes are heavy with sleep. They are closing. You are going to sleep, going to sleep, going . . . LOOK! JUST GO TO SLEEP, WILL YOU!' After ten minutes he was sleeping like a baby and Ralph and I were just debating what

without the nappy, obviously

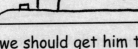

we should get him to do – Ralph was really keen for Aaron to pee out of the window – when there was a loud knock at the loo door.

'Aaron,' I whispered, 'listen. Obey my commands. Put on your Miss Bird voice and say the curry thing again to make the teacher go away.'

Aaron stood up like a robot and went to the door. 'Yes,' he said in his high-pitched Miss Bird voice. 'What's your problem, matey? I'm curri-fied again.'

'Who is this?' said the teacher at the loo door.

'Miss Bird,' said Aaron.

'That's funny,' said the voice. 'So am I.'

We had to reprogram Aaron quick.

'Stop doing Miss Bird,' I hissed. 'Do Mr Quinell.' He was the big sports master. Everyone was scared of him.

'Just having a joke, there,' said Aaron, switching to Mr Quinell's deep Welsh voice. 'I'm in here doing what men do, look

We would have gone out of the window again, but Mr Figgis (Physics), Mr Quinn (English) and Mr Ranakunda (History) were making steam clouds up against the wall.

you, Miss Bird. I'd be grateful for a little time alone. Shall we say ten minutes, because I've still got to pump up my balls! For football practice, of course—' Aaron would have gone on if Ralph hadn't put a hand over his mouth.

'Whoever you are in there,' said Miss Bird, 'I'm getting the headmistress.'

We heard her leave, then legged it through the door.

Running down the corridor, Aaron was still under the influence and still thought he was Mr Quinell. He wouldn't shut up about balls. 'Bet I've got more balls than you lot!' he shouted at a group of dinner ladies. 'If you come to the games cupboard,' he winked at a lost mother, 'I'll show you my balls!'

We rushed him past, but only into the path of three rather mean-looking Upper Sixth boys.

'I can do kick-ups with my balls,' Aaron cried. 'What can you nancy-boys do with yours?'

It was the wrong thing to say.

When Aaron came round he was out of the trance. 'Did it work?' he asked.

'You could say that,' I said.

'And you promise I didn't do anything stupid?'

I looked at Ralph and he looked at me. 'Nothing,' I said.

So it must have come as a bit of a shock to Aaron when he looked in the mirror and saw his throbbing black eye.

Revengers came home with me after school to doctor sofa. Mr E had second leg in plaster. If he was turned on his back and stuck to the table he'd make a good toast rack. *For one piece of toast.*

William told me that he wanted my sofa in half an hour. I told him he could have it, but only if I could practise hypnotism on him and Mel. He said no way, because he didn't trust me further than he could spit. I have seen how far William can spit. It dribbles down his chin.

We had thirty minutes to sabotage the sofa. Before we did, Ralph had the brilliant idea of practising kissing on it for the party.

'What with?' I asked.

'Anything soft,' he said.

So Aaron grabbed a pillow, Ralph grabbed a teddy bear and I grabbed an old pair of trousers. Then we took it in turns to roll around on the sofa making panting noises like we'd just run 400 metres. Aaron nearly suffocated himself in the pillow, Ralph stuck his tongue in the teddy's

I may be stuffed but I still have my pride

NO to Bear snogging

ear and got stuffing stuck between his teeth, and I was going well with the trousers till I caught my lip in the zip and now it's all swollen and tastes of Savlon.

After the kissing we removed the wooden

slats under the seat and hid them under my bed, so that I could mend the sofa when *I* wanted to use it. We had just put the cushions back, so that everything looked normal, when William breezed in and told the three of us to scram. Then he opened the window and helped Rosie climb in.

We sat outside on the landing, ignoring William and Rosie's cries for help. The man-eating sofa had collapsed as planned. They had fallen through the hole and the cushions had folded around them. It was as if a huge mouth had gobbled them up, leaving only their legs poking out between the lips!

At least, this was the sight that greeted Mum when she barged in to see what the screams were about. William got blasted for having a girl in the house without telling Mum, and Rosie was marched downstairs and sent home.

My big brother waited for the Revengers to leave before coming back into my room and breaking each of the

wooden slats across his knee. 'If I can't sit on your sofa, neither can you,' he said.

'I'll tell Mum what you've just done,' I said.

'No, you won't,' said William, miming the hole in the roof. It was a question of size, apparently, and his blackmail was bigger than mine. Also his fist was bigger than my head. Point taken.

Cornelius had been clearing trees so he joined us for supper. We had frozen pizza. Granny disapproved, of course, and said she was surprised we weren't all midgets thanks to the minuscule amount of goodness Mum put in our bodies! Mum told Granny that if she didn't like the food maybe she should cook tomorrow night and Granny said that she jolly well might. Personally I'd rather she went home and we ate cat food.

Do I have a Fairy Godmother? I think I might! Mr Stratford just turned up with his son Colin and three scaffolders. He'd only finished Granny's roof! That's 'finished' as in, 'The old moaner can go home now!'

Is that a choir of angels I hear singing, 'Hallelujah'?!

66

Mum hugged Cornelius. Cornelius hugged Mum. I hugged Mum. Mum hugged Mr Stratford. Cornelius hugged Mr Stratford. I hugged Cornelius and Cornelius hugged the scaffolders. Colin must have felt left out.

Not for long, though. Mel had rushed out of the room when he'd arrived and had now returned, wearing a much shorter skirt and cake-loads of make-up. 'Cup of coffee?' she said with pouty lips like a sink-plunger.

Colin's eyes

'I wouldn't say no to a cup of tea,' said Colin. 'Any biscuits?'

Mr Stratford is starting tomorrow. He told Mum that he could get everything fixed by Saturday so long as he and Colin worked flat out. Mum beamed and said to Granny, 'Constance, tomorrow you can go home.'

But Granny didn't want to go. She said she was too frightened. 'What if there's another storm?' she trembled. 'I'm only a little old lady. I'm too weak to cope on my own.' Then, while she hid the chocolate biscuits from Colin, Granny asked what Cornelius was doing with the scaffolders. He was outside kissing them and telling them they'd saved his party. They were big, beer-swilling men who looked like they couldn't wait to build their scaffolding and run up a ladder to safety.

So Granny is staying. It is now official. When Dad got home she made him tie her to her armchair then nail her to the sitting-room floor so she couldn't be picked up and chucked out while she was sleeping.

That's the armchair he nailed, not Granny.

*Cat Dracula has been hurling himself against the windows ever since.

Unfortunately Dad cut himself on a nail. The finger was spurting blood like a fire hydrant so Napoleon was locked outside as a life-saving precaution. *

There is only so much blood a daddy can lose before he becomes a mummy.

20:40 – Answered phone to Roger the Todger, but instead of rushing forward to snatch it out of my hand, Mel backed off. 'You speak to him,' she hissed. 'Tell him I don't ever want to see him again.'

'What?'

'Do it! Or I spill the roof-hole beans to Mum and Dad,' she said.

'She hates you,' I said. 'Go away!'

He started blubbing.

'Oh no. Now he's blubbing,' I said.

'Good,' she said. 'Let him wail.'

'He says he loves you,' I told her.

'Well tell him "I don't love you!"'

'I don't love you,' I said before hanging up.

Don't expect he loves me either.

69

THE MYSTERY THAT
iS BiG SiSTERS

Why would Mel suddenly go off Roger that quick? I don't get it.

20.55 — Help! Just remembered French worksheet. Will just have to dash it off and hope Miss Bird doesn't notice.

FRENCH WORKSHEET
Alistair Fury

Decline the verb ÊTRE
Je suis = I am Swiss
Tu eh = You what
Il est = I'm ill
Nous sums = know your times tables
View etre = To be seen
Ils son = They sing

Write a description of an important event on your last holiday to France
An Englishman was driving his car when he stopped for a French hitchhiker.
'Would you like a lift?' asked the English driver.

'Oui oui,' said the French hitchhiker.
'Not in my car you don't,' said the Englishman.

What is the most important French City?
Le capital de France est Paris, may le capital de Paris est P.

In your own words, describe what makes France French

A STORY ABOUT FRANCE
By Alistair Fury

Unce upon un temp, there was a snail, qui avez un race with un tortoise. The gun va pouf! The race avez commenced. It took beaucoup beaucoup beaucoup days to finish. Not becop they were both si slow, but becop les French peeps avez eaten them. Voila. This est just comme les French are!

Write down five phrases in common usage and translate into English
Bonjovi, j'apple Alistair — Hello I'm called Alistair
Je vienna Tooting — I come from Tooting but I live in Vienna
J'ai pleur — I am feeling rainy

merde! - Oh crikey!
Toujours toujours - Enough already

Write a poem in French
MON FRAIR EST CACA
Frair est caca, frair est caca
Smelly poo, smelly poo
Doggy Mel's a meanie, doggy Mel's a meanie
Ding dang pong, ding dang pong.

Find out as many facts about France as you can

THE FRENCH REPUBLIC
Area: 543,965 Sq km
Population: 58,109,000
Capital: Paris
Population of Paris: 2,152,300
Religion: Roman Catholic
Language: French
Literacy: 99%
Life expectancy: 78 years
Industrial Economy: Iron and steel;
machinery; transportation equipment; elec-
tronics; chemicals; textiles; food
processing; uranium
Export Crops: Livestock, wheat, dairy
products, wine, fruits, vegetables

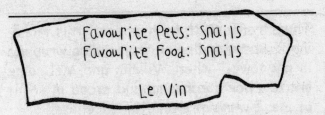

Favourite Pets: Snails
Favourite Food: Snails

Le Vin

What is the point of knowing these facts? I am not a better person for it. There can only be one reason why I am being forced to learn them. Because a certain beaky-nosed French teacher is trying to murder her least favourite pupil by boring me to death!

22.35 – Bonsai.

WEDNESDAY

The strangest thing happened this morning. I was standing on the landing wrapped in my towel* when William and Mel came out of their bedrooms and stood in front of me. I was not expecting niceness.

*The landing wasn't wrapped in my towel - that would be a huge towel

'We've done wrong, Alistair,' said Mel. 'And we're sorry.'

I was struck dumb.

'We want to make it up to you,' said William. 'I mean, after all, we are brothers and sisters.'

'Like that family in *The Sound of Music*,' said Mel.

'You want us to be nice to each other like the Von Trapp family?' I said in a moment of panic.

'That's them,' she said.

'You want us to wear clothes made out of flowery curtains?'

'Forget curtains. Forget slavery,' said Will. 'Mel and I want to do something for *you* for a change.'

I pinched myself to check I wasn't dreaming. 'Is this a wind-up?' I asked.

'No,' he said. 'We know you're interested in hypnotism and it can't be easy finding victims, and you *did* ask us yesterday . . . So we'd like to say yes.'

74

'Wow!' I said. 'Thank you.' But behind the smile I was really thinking: Right, suckers, this is payback time!

'There's one condition,' said William.

'What's that?' I said.

'You won't do anything nasty to us, will you?'

'No, no, no, no, no, no, no, no, no,' I said. 'No.'

'You promise?' said Mel.

'Of course,' I said.

'And you won't turn us into pets?'

'No, it works on humans too.'

'OK,' they said. 'Off you go.'

They wanted to do it in Mel's room. So I

put them to sleep by counting down from a hundred with the Floating Finger of Forty Winks. Then, just to test they were 'under', I asked them to say out loud what they thought of their *lovely* brother Alistair. I stressed the word 'lovely'.

'He is lovely,' said William.

'Yes, lovely,' said Mel.

This was easier than stealing sweets from a baby. I got bold. I said, 'Right, you two, here's the way it is.'

'Woof!' said William.

'Miaow,' said Mel.

For one awful moment I thought I'd turned them into pets, but it was just a blip. Next thing I knew they were smiling peacefully again and William said, 'Carry on, Great Guru.'

'Oh yes,' said Mel. 'Fill us with your wisdom.'

'Right,' I said. 'Get this! You have for-gotten everything you saw on the roof

where Alistair made that hole with his clumsy feet. It never happened. It was the hurricane. And from this day forth you shall love your little brother, never make him your slave again and buy him presents all the time with your own money. And I mean big presents. Nod your heads if you understand.' They both nodded. 'Oh, and if Giselle is pretty when she gets here you have to make sure she kisses me. That's it. You can come out now!' And they opened their eyes and rubbed them. 'Well?' I said. 'How do you feel?'

'We should ask you that,' said William.

'Why?' I asked.

'Because we weren't asleep, meathead!' Mel produced the video camera they'd set up to film me. 'And now we've got your confession on tape, so now you're more our slave than ever before!'

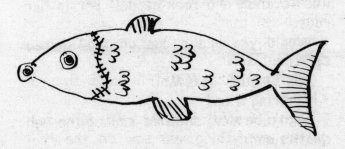

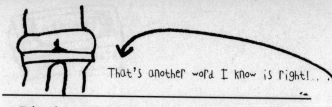

That's another word I know is right!...

I had just been stitched up like a kipper.

'We just thought,' explained William, 'what with the booby-trapped sofa, that maybe you were getting a little too big for your boots. So, just in case you're getting any ideas about blackmailing *us*, this tape is a reminder that *we* are blackmailing *you*. OK?'

Bum! Or, as they say in France, *Burm!*

Mr Stratford and Colin were already drinking tea when I got down for breakfast. Mel was wearing that short skirt again. Suddenly she put her hand across her forehead and swooned. 'I don't think I'm very well,' she squeaked. 'I can't go to school.'

Mum thought she looked fine. Granny thought she'd probably caught a cold from not having any clothes on. Mel insisted she was feverish and took herself off to her room.

'Would you like a cup of tea?' asked Colin.

'Yes I would,' said Mel.

'I'll bring it up.'

'That'd be nice,' she said, smiling through death's door.

Seconds later, she and Colin came back down again.

'Colin's going to the builder's shop and said he'll take me to the doctor,' said Mel.

'I need sandpaper,' he said.

'But what about the work on the house—?'

Mum's cry was answered by the slam of the front door. 'Oh dear. Can you manage without him?' she asked Mr Stratford.

'I can only do what I can do,' he said ominously. Then he went outside and climbed the scaffolding, while Cornelius appeared in a pair of leather shorts fringed with tassels.

'What are you staring at?' he said. 'Bondi Beach arrives this morning. These are my sand-shovelling shorts!'

At school, Miss Bird raised her head from my French worksheet and looked at me like

He has, but not living with him.

a vet looks at a horse with a broken leg – I'm sorry, Dobbin, but it's best for everyone if I shoot you. 'Tomorrow morning,' she said, 'you will welcome the French exchange students in assembly with a short but fluent speech expressing your admiration for the French nation and the many virtues of the British, and of course you will do it all in French!'

'Quoi?' I said. 'Moi? Sacré beurre!'

Aaron came up with a genius plan so we wouldn't be disturbed in the teachers' loos at lunchtime. We hung a sign on the door saying:

OUT OF ORDER – STICKY LOCK
CROSS YOUR LEGS TILL YOU GET HOME OR
DO IT IN A BOTTLE

'I've worked out why we don't know any girls,' Aaron said. 'It must be because of us. Ralph's too good looking. I haven't got a father. And Alistair plays the piano.' There wasn't much Ralph or Aaron could do about their problems, but I didn't have to play the piano. 'Girls think boys who play the piano are cissies,' said Aaron, 'which means that they think we're cissies too, because Ralph and me are your best mates.'

'It's as bad as being a ballet dancer,' said Ralph.

'Not a problem,' I said. 'I want to give up piano anyway. Mrs Muttley or, as I prefer to call her, Plague-Woman, is the most disgusting person I have ever met. She has more diseases than a medieval hospital and every week she shows them to me! Boils, bunions, septic veruccas! They make me want to be sick. Her runny eye looks like thin custard, her liquid ear glows in the dark and her breath is so full of toxic germs that she could spot-weld warships with it!'

'Why don't you wear a gas mask?' said Aaron.

Aaron must be eating tons of fish these days, because his brain just seems to get bigger and bigger.

'I tried it once, but couldn't read the music when the goggles fogged up!' I said. 'But worst of all are the wiggly warts on her hands, because she's always touching my fingers with hers and I shall catch them. I shall be known as Alis*toad* Fury and small children will cross the road when they see me approaching!'

Luckily I had a lesson that afternoon so I could tell her I was finished with her then, but it wasn't going to be easy. Then Aaron had a brilliant idea to get *Mum* to tell Mrs Muttley for me.

'Pretend you've got warts,' he said. 'Tell your mum you caught them off Mrs

Warts on the loose

Muttley and she'll never let you go back in case you catch more!'

We called the mission Operation Wart Trap, and before I went off to engage with the enemy, Ralph and Aaron shook my hand.

'This may be the last time we'll ever do this,' said Aaron. 'In case you catch something, I mean.'

'Good luck, soldier,' said Ralph.

To create the wart effect, I stuck Rice Krispies on the back of my hands with glue then painted them pink and brown for that authentic warty appearance. Was worried that Mum might not notice my hands so added a few more around my eyes until it looked like I was wearing wart spectacles. Heard Mum's voice in the sitting room and went straight in. 'Mum,' I said, 'I've caught warts.'

She leapt up from the chair when she saw my face. 'Alistair!' she screamed.

I was suddenly aware that Mum was not

alone. Behind me stood Dad, Granny, Cornelius, Mel, William and a girl I'd never met before. Long black hair, big smile, huge eyes, quite big ears, but not too big. It was Giselle. She was really beautiful. And there was me with warts the size of barnacles!

Everyone was staring at me. William laughed. Granny dropped her cup of tea and Cornelius fell back onto the sofa clutching his heart. I had to say something or I'd have looked even more of a fool. 'Bonjovi,' I said to Giselle. 'Welcome a Tooting.'

'What has happened to you?' gasped Mum.

'You look hideous,' howled William. 'Giselle, this is my baby brother, Alice.'

'I am not a baby,' I told her. 'And my name is Alistair! I'm a boy!' It was vital she knew.

'Warts?' said my mum. 'Where did they come from?'

Now this was the point in Operation Wart Trap where I should have blown my music teacher away. If I'd said, 'From Mrs Muttley,' I'd never have had to go back again. But admit to *warts* in front of

84

Giselle? Never!

'Did you say "warts"!' I said. 'Ha! Of course I haven't got warts.' I picked one off my face and ate it, causing Mel to retch into a vase. 'No, these are painted Rice Krispies,' I said, rubbing the back of my hands and sprinkling the carpet. 'It was a joke.'

Now I had to think of a convincing lie. 'I was pretending to be . . .' Come on brain, think! What was I pretending to be with lumps of cereal stuck to my face? '. . . a frog,' I said, '. . . with lumpy skin and that, to make Giselle feel at home.' I wanted to die. Of all the things to call her on our first meeting, I'd called her a frog!

Dear God,
Please make Giselle's English as bad as my French, then she won't have understood.
Love, Alistair

On the way out Giselle waved at me and said, 'Goodbye frog-boy.'

Brilliant! She's intelligent as well as beautiful. Just my luck!

I washed the warts off, because warts had brought me noughts. Of joy, that is.

I decided to hypnotize Mrs Muttley into letting me give up piano.

Lesson got off to a typically disgusting start. She patted my hand with her warts. 'Today will be your last lesson before Saturday's concert, Alistair.'

'Mrs Muttley,' I said, 'about your warts . . .'

'I've tried chopping them off with a cheese grater,' she said, 'but it's no good. They've dug their little roots in.'

'I can get rid of them,' I said. 'By hypnotism.'

Took ten minutes to get her to sleep using the arm of her metronome. To test if she was under my spell I said this: 'I hope you are asleep, Mrs Muttley, because I'm going to put a crocodile in your blouse right now!' I wasn't really.

Phew!

Her eyes stayed closed so I got to the point. 'Now hear this, you creepy reptile. Music is stopping Alistair Fury from becoming a man. So he's going and never coming back. Accept this. Do not weep. He will never play piano again, because he hates it. Accept this. Do not weep. He thinks you're fairly horrible, actually, with your diseases. So he won't be coming back. He won't even be walking past your front door in case he catches something. Accept this. Do not weep. And he hates Chopin too. When you wake up, you will feel refreshed and kittenish and bear no hatred towards Alistair Fury, but you will *never* want him back. You will only wish him well in his pursuit of girls. That's your lot. Over and out. Snap out of it!'

But that was just so he could hold her hand and stroke it.

She came round with a huge intake of breath and a splutter of spittle. 'You can go home now,' she said. 'I think we both know you don't like it here.' Then she let out a howl like a wolf, but obviously didn't realize she'd done it. 'Goodbye, Alistair Fury.' As I was leaving she tousled my hair.

Ran home. Washed evil wart juice out of my hair then rushed downstairs to see Giselle, but William was there first.

'I want to see how a normal English family lives,' she was saying. 'In France, people think English are bad cooks, but your mother is on TV! Cool!'

William told her that he was a great sportsman, but that didn't seem to impress her. So he told her that she had beautiful eyes. 'Like two green gooseberries,' he said, 'with a fleck of blue in the corner just like a tiny lump of mould. In other words, gooseberries that have sat in the basket too long and attracted fruit flies.' She wasn't too impressed by this either, so he lied and said he could read palms.

Meanwhile I sat there saying nothing, my mind a blank, my mouth fixed in a smile. I had never spoken to a girl before and didn't know what she wanted me to say.

ooh La La!

Eventually, after she'd been smiling back at me for an age, I found the right words. 'So France has a population of fifty-eight million, one hundred and nine thousand,' I said casually. 'Do you know many of them?'

William pushed me out of the door and told me to go play with the traffic.

'And good riddance!' shouted Granny. 'Now I can hear the racing!'

So *that* was the point of learning French facts! Never again would I be lost for words in front of Giselle. I ran upstairs and re-learned all the other facts off my worksheet so that I would look intelligent next time I spoke to her.

Just before supper Mel came back from the doctor's.

'So where's your medicine?' Dad asked.

'I didn't need any,' she said.

'Why not?' said Mum.

'Because I was waiting so long, I felt better by the time I saw the doctor.'

'So where's Colin been all day?' Mum said.

'He had to go further than normal for sandpaper,' she said.

'Where to?' said Mum. 'Leeds? If this kitchen isn't ready for my party, Melanie, it'll be his fault.'

Mum produced dust-covered scampi and chips for supper. Giselle obviously hated it, because she retched and pushed it to the side of her plate.

I leaned across and said, 'I expect this is not as nice as snails, Giselle, which is the most popular dish in France, I believe. And they make such lovely pets, too, don't you agree? Very cuddly.'

sorry I'm twenty eight years late... I took the snail for a WALK

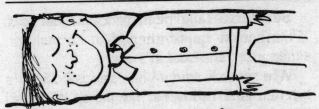

She moved her chair away from me.

22.08 – William moved into my room and took the bed. I was put on the sofa, which was like sleeping in a Venus Flytrap or wearing a straitjacket instead of pyjamas. I sank into the hole and my arms were pinned to my sides by the cushions. I couldn't move. All I could do was think. So I thought quite a lot about how much I liked Giselle.

22.20 – Woken by phone ringing. Heard it picked up. Then suddenly William backed into the room, put his finger to his lips and shut the door so no-one else could hear him. 'Of course I love you, Rosie,' he whispered. 'I wouldn't be going out with you if I didn't, would I?'

'Do you mind?' I said. 'I'm trying to sleep.'

He said goodbye to Rosie, then stood in front of my face with his legs apart.

'Why don't you want Giselle to know that you've got a girlfriend?' I asked.

'Because Giselle might fancy me,' he said. 'I don't want to put her off.'

'So just tell Rosie it's over.'

'Are you kidding!' he said. 'Rosie's a nutter. If I tell her it's finished she'll kill me. And if she gets to find out that there's another girl involved she'll do worse! She made it clear when we first went out that if I ever cheated on her she would pour a tin of red paint over my head!'

'Then leave Giselle alone,' I said. It seemed simple enough to me, but obviously not to William.

'Playing the field is not simple, Alice. Being in love with two girls at the same time requires sophisticated thinking. But then, I wouldn't expect you to understand, because you're just a child!' Then he turned round, bent forward and knocked me out with an evil ripsnorter right between my eyes.

23.45 – Have just come round with a headache. Granny *must* go home tomorrow. Another night of William's farts and my brain will melt.

23.47 – A poem has just decomposed itself in my head

Bonsai Giselle

Giselle, Giselle, Giselle, Giselle,
I deja like you more than Mel.

00.34 – Cannot sleep. The sheer un-comfortableness of this sabotaged sofa is making my dreams get quite a lot weirder.

MY GETTING QUITE A LOT WEIRDER DREAM

I am walking Mr E in the park when three strange dogs run out of the bushes looking for trouble. These dogs have got four legs like normal dogs, but their heads are William, Rosie and Giselle's! Then I pick up a stick and throw it miles and the William, Rosie and Giselle dogs give chase followed by Mr E. And all four dive into a pond to fetch the stick, but only two come up – Mr E and Giselle. And then the Giselle dog thanks me for getting rid of the William and Rosie dogs. Only she's not a dog any more, she's a real girl and she's kissing me! And it's all warm and wet and sloppy!

06.38 – Woke with smile on face. My dream kiss was a beautiful experience. The real kiss was revolting. As a cracking joke, William had sat Mr E on my chest and made him lick my mouth. That is *Mr E* – a dirty little dog who licks his own bottom! I soaped my tongue three times to get rid of the germs!

This picture of Mr E licking his bum is FAR too horrid to be shown and is nothing at all to do with it being difficult to draw - so there.

07.55 – Giselle and William went off to school early and missed the big scene.

Overnight, Mel had developed claustrophobia. This meant she couldn't stay in small rooms for any length of time. So she couldn't go to school and couldn't stay at home. Cinemas were OK, apparently, as were department stores and burger restaurants. So that was where she was going to spend her day.

'I'm not sure,' said Mum suspiciously. 'I

think you should go to school and see how you feel.'

To which Mel's response was to burst into tears. 'The walls! The walls!' she cried dramatically. 'The walls are closing in on me!' She just *had* to get out! Just as Colin

SLAM!

I wish they would

had to drive down to the builder's shop for more sandpaper and take Mel with him. And Mr Stratford just *had* to re-plaster the ceiling, re-tile the wall, re-lay the floor and re-decorate the whole kitchen all on his own.

Cornelius turned up just as Mr Stratford was having a quiet word with Mum and Dad. I asked Cornelius if he wanted to see how little work had been done, but he said he didn't, because he'd just done his mascara and didn't want it running down his cheeks.

Meanwhile Mum was crying for both of them. Mr Stratford was telling her that he couldn't finish on time unless he had more money for more men. Mum blamed Colin for never being there. Dad offered himself as a worker if Mr Stratford thought it would speed things up.

'This is not *Changing Rooms*!' snapped Mum. 'Whatever you might think, you are NOT Handy Andy!'

Dad said he was only trying to help, then he slammed outside to fiddle with his barbecue, while Mum grabbed Mr Stratford's lapels.

'This party has to be perfect!' she said. 'I will pay you the extra money, just don't tell my husband.'

Before assembly I called a secret meeting of the Revengers in the playground. 'I'll suffocate if I don't get William and his farts back into his own bedroom,' I said. 'So I think we should do some instant evil revenges on Granny so that she won't want to stay with us any more.'

'Like what?' said Aaron.

'I haven't given this much thought, obviously,' I said, 'but we could blindfold her, lead her up to a pelican crossing and tell her that she can only walk when she hears the beeps. Then while the little man is still red, we make beep beep beep noises

behind her back!' Ralph and Aaron stared at me, horrified. 'All right, maybe we should choose less fatal revenges,' I said, 'like making her a cup of tea with dirty dishwater or undoing a Custard Cream, scraping out the custard and slapping lard inside instead.'

But Ralph wasn't comfortable. 'We can't scare off a granny,' he said. 'It's not right. She's too old and feeble.'

'How about hypnotism?' said Aaron.

'No,' I said. 'You can't hypnotize someone who's always asleep. And if she's awake she'll just ask rude questions, because that's what she does.'

The bell rang for assembly and stopped the meeting. Will just have to find a different way to send Granny packing.

Stood up in front of whole school and gave my welcome speech to French exchange students. Miss Bird must have been very happy. She wanted to humiliate me and it worked.

'Mes ducks and mon sewers, hello to les students de Franch. They will be sad ici, becop Franch est un country where il y a beaucoup de snails. Il y a snails dans le bain, et il y a snails dans la maison, et if it's not il y a snails, it est frurgs. Frurgs' legs et snails are la feesh and cheeps de Franch. But il y a no snails in Englanterra, so les students de Franch will be sad. Oh yes. The capital de Franch est Paris et le population de Paris est two million, one hundred and fifty-two thousand three hundred. Bonsai.'

Everyone laughed at me when I walked back to my seat in the hall. William punched me on the arm for being so embarrassing, but Giselle stood up and kissed me on the cheeks. Both of them. That was TWO kisses! One after the other, as if she liked the first one so much that instantly she came back for more! I daren't write the word in case I'm fooling myself, but I think she might f***y me!

'Brave,' she said. 'Very brave.'

On her way out from assembly Giselle walked past Ralph, Aaron and me. Ralph had been quiet and smiley since he'd seen her kiss me. Suddenly he stepped out in front of her. 'Hello,' he said. 'I'm Ralph.' He kept forgetting to blink. Aaron looked much the same, like they were the Gormless Twins, only Aaron seemed to have lockjaw too. He couldn't speak.

'And this is Aaron,' I said.

Then both of them exploded with laughter and Ralph left a slug of gob on his chin. Then they stopped laughing. Then they went red.

'So France has an area of five hundred and forty-three thousand, nine hundred and sixty-five square kilometres,' I said. 'That is big. So Giselle, what do you like?'

'Pardon?' she said.

'What do you l i k e ? Football, knitting, guillo-tining?'

'Oh,' she said. 'I don't like s p o r t . Too angry. But I love to play the piano. My favourite composer is Chopin.'

I had a mad rush of blood to the head. 'Chopin!' I cried. 'Quelle luck! He's *my* favourite composer as well. In fact I'm playing him on Saturday at a concert!' Even before the words were out, I knew I was in trouble.

At break Ralph couldn't get those kisses out of his mind. 'I wonder if she'd kiss me as well?' he said.

'She kissed Alistair because she felt sorry for him,' said Aaron. 'So she'd have to have a good reason for doing it.'

'Yeah, like fancying me!' said Ralph.

'No way,' said Aaron. 'A *real* reason.'

'Like being at our party!' said Ralph, getting all excited. 'Don't you see, we don't need any other girls. We just ask Giselle.'

'Why?'

'Because she's an expert kisser.'

'How do you know that?'

'Because she's French!' he said. 'I think I love her.'

'You don't even know her,' I said. 'Anyway, other people might love her too.'

'You mean *you*, don't you?' said Aaron. 'What's brought this on?'

'Kissing the dog,' I told him. 'I didn't realize it was the dog, obviously. But it was lovely.' Then I said, 'Anyway I saw her first!' And Ralph couldn't argue with that.

We decided that we couldn't ask Giselle on her own, because it might look a bit obvious. So Ralph's going to ask his little sister and Aaron's got a nine-year-old cousin who looks older in make-up.

'You know what's going to swing this for us?' said Ralph. 'Alistair's piano.' He reckoned that Giselle and me sharing a mutual love of piano playing would be the key to her accepting our invite, but this left me with a big doubt.

'She'll never come to our party now,' I said. 'When she finds out I'm not playing in the concert on Saturday she'll know I'm a liar. And nobody likes a liar.'

But the others thought I was being too gloomy. All I had to do was make sure I *was* in the concert by unhypnotizing Mrs Muttley and sucking up to her big-time! *

Because of William's phone call last night and his obvious interest in Giselle, we decided to have the party on Sunday night at Aaron's, because that was the night William was taking Rosie to his rugby

* This would not under any circumstances involve the kissing of hands!

party, and that would put him out the picture!

It was my job to ask Giselle to the party, but I didn't want it. I didn't have the right words and I was too embarrassed. 'What if she says no?' I said. 'If she laughs at me I'll probably never be able to talk to another girl in my life.'

Ralph gave me some advice. 'She won't say no,' he said, 'if you treat her like a lady and say nice things about her.'

'Like what?' I said.

'Like this,' said Ralph, crossing his arms over his chest in a lover's pose.

British Beef and French Mustard,
Go together like snails and custard.
You and I might very well be,
Love childs of the European Community.

'I see,' I said, but inside I was twisted up with jealousy. Why couldn't I think of something as beautiful as that?

I was nervous about going back to see Mrs Muttley. If she rejected me my life might never be the same again. I needed courage and turned to the inspirational words of wisdom of the very great Nelson Mandela: 'To do nothing is to be dead, but to struggle is to feel alive!' Or was it Stone Cold Steve Austin from WWF Wrestling?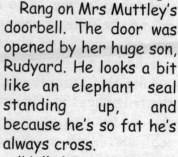

Or, as the French say, courage

It was the wrestler. Anyway, it's true.

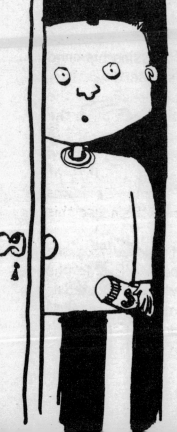

Rang on Mrs Muttley's doorbell. The door was opened by her huge son, Rudyard. He looks a bit like an elephant seal standing up, and because he's so fat he's always cross.

'Hello,' I said. 'Is Mrs Muttley in?'

'No,' he said. 'Hospital.'

I panicked and said, 'Nothing to do with her mind, I hope.'

'No,' said Rudyard, 'her bum.'

It was nice to see that he'd inherited his mother's lack of embar-

rassment. I got the name of the hospital, a list of visiting times and a look at Rudyard's appendix, which he always carries in his pocket in a little plastic jar.

Ran home. On the doorstep Napoleon cocked his leg against my trousers. I clicked my fingers and hissed, 'Stop being a dog, you're a cat!' but he obviously didn't understand. When I went indoors he was dancing the Bump with my ankle.

Mr E was lying on Granny's lap in the sitting room with the *Racing Post* propped against his plaster-casted legs. She had the horse-racing on the telly and was fast asleep. Mr Stratford was working on the roof, and was the only other person in the house. Mum and Cornelius had gone off to meet the Two Rolfs and Dad had popped down the sawmill to chop up big bits of tree. I was alone with Granny. If I was ever going to get her out of the house this was my moment!

I had to think fast. I checked that she really was asleep, chucked Mr E onto the sofa, then ran into the garden and shouted up at Mr Stratford. 'Mr Stratford! Come quick! I need your help! I think Granny Constance is dead and needs the Kiss of Life.'

Not very bright

Mr Stratford   A dim bulb

We rushed into the sitting room, with me urging Mr Stratford to save her life with a smacker. He plunged towards her, their lips met and I took a photo.

'What are you doing?' he said.

'First Aid training,' I said, tearing the instant print out of the camera. 'I have to prove that I've been present at a Kiss of

Life Demonstration. Now I have. Thank you.'

The fool actually believed me and went back to his roof!

Then I woke Granny up with a cup of tea.

'Sleep well?' I said, keeping it chummy before I slipped the knife in. 'Oh, by the way, look what I've found, Granny.' I showed her the photo of her snogging the builder. 'Wasn't it lucky that *I* found it first and not Mummy or Daddy, or one of the Scrabble Club, or Mrs Stratford, or even the editor of the *Tooting Tribune*!'

She packed her bags right away and announced that she was leaving.

'Was it something I said?' I said.

'I know when I'm not wanted,' said Granny. 'And I won't require any help with my things, thank you, Alistair. I shall manage them on my own, just as I have managed *everything* on my own since I've been here!'

I still had to carry her suitcases to the

taxi. Then, after the taxi had gone I wheeled the armchair and TV round to her house.

'You're sneaky,' she smiled. Then shut the door.

I had just moved William out of my bedroom when I heard the front door open and Dad moaning in the hall. Got downstairs to find him slumped on the sofa with his right hand in a bandage and Napoleon licking his bloodstained fingers like they were lollies. He'd caught his fingers in the circular saw, apparently, which must have given everyone at the sawmill a really good laugh.

Mel came back with Colin. She had grass stains on the back of her jumper from being in a field all day – to combat the claustrophobia. Then Mum and Cornelius returned. Actually, it was a good job they came back when they did, because Dad had accidentally sat on Mr E. A weary Mum took him back to the Blue Cross Hospital.

'Oh, that's nice,' said Dad. 'You take the *dog* to hospital but you don't take *me!*'

'*You've* still got two legs to walk on,' she said, 'which is more than can be said for Mr E.'

18.05 – Concern. Why are Mum and Dad so snappy at the moment? It's not as if they're under any pressure. I mean, it's only a *party* on Sunday, and it's only a *tiny* hole in the roof. I'd like to see how they'd cope under real pressure, like asking Giselle to a party.

19.20 – I've been trying to avoid Giselle all evening, because every time I see her I know I should ask her, but I can't, so I feel like a coward. Then after supper there was a knock on my bedroom door and she came in. This was the perfect opportunity, but I couldn't do it. It was like I was asking, 'Giselle, would you like to stick your head in a mincer on Sunday night?' Or, 'Giselle, would you like to poison your entire family with mad cow moo-burgers?' Each time I

Is zeez ok for you Alistair?

Mince-o-matic

Mind you, I don't think she knew that wine was one of France's main exports. So not all is lost.

opened my mouth to ask her, the only thing that came out was another stupid fact about France.

She didn't want to talk about France any more. She said she was feeling homesick and wanted to listen to me playing Chopin instead.

'Come to the concert on Saturday,' I said. 'Listen then!'

But she wanted to listen *now* and sat down on the sofa before I could stop her.

'Sorry,' I said, as I pulled her from the sofa's jaws. 'It always does that.'

'I'm OK,' she said. 'What about Chopin?'

'Chopin,' I said, trying to brazen it out while I thought of an excuse. 'Or as I prefer to call him, Chop-In! Ha!' I sat down and cracked my knuckles like I was warming up.

'No music?' she said.

'No,' I said. 'Don't need it. Know it by heart.' Then I cleared my throat, rubbed my nose, pulled my ear and said, 'Did you hear that?'

'No,' she said. 'What?'

'Mum telling me to go to bed.'

'It's only seven thirty!' she said.

'But it's Friday,' I said.

110

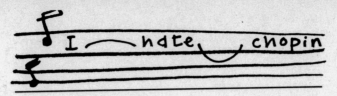

'No, Thursday.'

'That's right. It's Friday *tomorrow* so that means today is Thursday, and Thursday's always early-to-bed night because ... erm ...' I didn't have a clue what I was going to say next. '... because Mum and Dad always have sex on Thursdays,' I said. 'You know, really embarrassing stuff. Would you be surprised if I told you that they weren't virgins?'

'Sex?' said Giselle.

'It's disgusting! Best get to bed right away before the walls start shaking. I'm so sorry. I'll play Chopin for you some other time,' I said, ushering her out of the room. 'Night!'

Horror! I'd forgotten I'd said that Chopin was my favourite! I hate his music and can't play any of it!

LIAR, LIAR, AL'S ON FIRE!

What am I going to do? I will go to her and tell her the truth.

19.56 – Giselle has gone to a bar with William. He has left me a note:

Alice. I AM A HOLEY MAN, BECAUSE I KNOW ABOUT THE HOLE. Nobody must ever know ABOUT TONIGHT, especially not Rosie.

23.48 – Knocked on guestroom door. A sleepy Giselle opened it. 'Ah, the liar,' she said. 'You have something to say to me?'

'I do,' I said, trying to pluck up courage. 'Would you ... erm ... Would you ... Would you believe that the life expectancy of your average Frenchman is seventy-eight years?'

She shut the door in my face.

oh, you know what I mean

OTHER THINGS TO DO TODAY
(APART FROM GETTING BACK INTO THE
CONCERT AND LEARNING TO PLAY CHOPIN
TO MAKE GISELLE SAY YES TO ME WHEN I
ASK HER TO OUR PARTY)
1) Ask Giselle to party
2) Ask Giselle to party
3) Ask Giselle to party
4) Ask Giselle to party

07.24 – Tried talking to Giselle to make her like me again. I told her that literacy in France was 99 per cent and that wheat and dairy products were two of France's main export crops, but that didn't do the trick. She still thinks I'm a liar.

Cornelius turned up wearing a bathing cap and a pair of swimming trunks. 'I thought the waiters could wear this,' he said. 'What do you think?'

'Lovely,' said Mum. 'Very Bondi.'

Cornelius then produced a surfboard from his car and brought it through for approval, passing a puzzled Giselle on the way.

'What is wrong with this country?' she said. 'In France it rains, yes, but not enough to go surfing in the garden!'

Colin must have brought extra sandpaper with him this morning, because he didn't need to drive to the builder's shop to buy some. He was outside in the garden when we left for school. Mr Stratford was up on the roof and Mum was saying, 'Shouldn't you be up there helping, Colin?'

'No,' he said. 'I'll only get in his way. Can I have another cup of tea, Mrs F?' Then he turned to Dad and said, 'So how's the barbecue coming on, then?'

'Not even remotely funny,' growled Dad.

That was our cue to leg it.

Mel came to school with the rest of us. Suspect she might have a genuine fever and doesn't know what she's doing. On the way, however, she backtracked and told us to go on without her.

Relieved to see Aaron in the playground. I needed advice urgently. How could I ask Giselle to the party when she thought I was a liar?

'You'll have to prove you *can* play Chopin,' he said.

'After I've got back into the concert?'

'That's right,' he said.

'But I can't!' I said. 'I really *can't* play Chopin!'

'Then we'll just have to cheat,' said Aaron, 'or we'll lose her.'

Just then Ralph turned up wearing pongy aftershave, red socks and Brylcreem in his hair. He looked like he'd just walked through a car wash. Asked him what he thought he looked like and got a rather sharp reply.

'Did Julia Roberts get where she is today by letting her moustache grow?' Obviously not. 'Did Jean-Claude Van Damme become one of the leading exponents of martial arts movies by losing

control of his hair?' Obviously not. 'Did John Travolta get the fit girl in *Grease*?'

'Well, yes,' I said.

'Then that's what I'm doing,' said Ralph. 'Grooming. Making the most of myself.'

'Making the most enormous *tit* of yourself,' snorted Aaron, as Giselle wandered over.

'Hello, liar,' she said to me. Ralph just grinned and grunted and lifted his arms to give her a whiff of his body spray. 'What IS that bad smell?' she said. 'It smells like cheap *parfum*, the sort boys wear to make them feel like men. How you say, eau de toilet.'

'Toilette,' said Ralph.

'Trust me,' said Giselle. 'You smell like an old potty.'

What are old people doing in trees in the first place? Are they so poor they have to eat leaves? Or do they all have tree-climbing pug dogs? Or maybe they sit in trees waiting to die, because then their journey to heaven is quicker.

What incredible luck! A siren went off in middle of first lesson. It was a flood warning, because of all the heavy rain. The school was evacuated and everyone was sent home for the weekend, except the rowing club who were shoved out in their canoes to rescue old people from trees.

Ralph and Aaron ran with me to Mrs Muttley's hospital. We agreed that I should get back into the concert first before worrying about learning to play Chopin. We'd just gone past the barber's shop and were turning into that road where that frogman was found in the skip when Aaron happened to look through the window of the pub. He stopped us with a cry and a pointed finger. Sitting snugly in the corner, drinking lager and tossing peanuts into each other's mouths, were Mel and Colin!

By the time we reached the hospital we had worked out just how valuable this information was to us:

1) If the work in the kitchen is not finished on time, Mum will not have her launch party and her career will be over.
2) Mum and Dad will blame Colin missing work every day for the kitchen not being finished on time.
3) Mel is responsible for Colin missing work!

Therefore Mel is responsible for the work in the kitchen not being finished on time, no launch party and the end of Mum's career. Got her!

TO MEL

Yes you should be
Very scared
You're about to be
Alistaired!

When I entered the ward, Mrs Muttley was sitting on a huge black rubber inner tube reading *Hello!* 'Ohhh!' she squealed when she saw me. 'Why are *you* here? I thought you never wanted to see me again.' Unfortunately I'd done a good job with the hypnotizing.

'Whatever gave you that idea?' I lied, pointing to the inner tube. 'Are you learning to swim or have you got a tractor parked outside?'

'Don't be silly,' she said. 'This is for my haemorrhoids. So I don't sit on them.'

'You know your concert . . .' I said quickly, getting off the subject before it turned grisly.

'The one you won't be playing in, because you hate playing the piano even more than you loathe me and my diseases?' she said.

'That's the one,' I winced. I had been thorough. 'Look, can I show you some-

thing?' I showed her my hypnotic finger. In less than a minute she was asleep. In less than five I'd turned her mind round. Then I asked the question again: 'Mrs Muttley, can I come back and play in the concert on Saturday?'

She beamed at me, held out her warty hands and said, 'Yes. But you'll be playing on your own, I'm afraid, because I've had to cancel it.'

The news knocked the puff out of me. 'Why?' I cried.

'It's the stabbing pain from the haemorrhoids,' she said. 'I don't have the strength, Alistair.'

Before I knew it I was crying and begging her to reconsider. A nurse put her hand on my shoulder. 'Don't worry,' she said. 'Your mother's going to be fine.'

Mother! How could anyone think that Plague-Woman was my *mother*! Maybe the nurse thought I wasn't a boy at all, but one of her warts – a particularly large one with independent spirit!

'Please don't cancel the concert,' I begged. 'It's the creative high spot of my year!'

Then I told Mrs Muttley how I'd been

practising every hour of every day to play a new piece by Chopin, and she said, 'I'm going to change. For too long I have selfishly inflicted my diseases on others. In future I shall wear rubber gloves to keep my warts under wraps.' Then she clasped me to her bosom and kissed my face all over.

Giselle had better be worth all this.

The bosom of death

'There's just one thing,' she said. 'I'm weak, Alistair. If I'm to get through this concert I'm going to need a lovely assistant.'

'Assistant?' I said warily.

'To help me on,' she said. 'And at the end, to give me a big bunch of flowers and a kiss.'

'Oh, another kiss,' I laughed with a false and cheesy grin. 'Is that entirely necessary?'

'It's vital,' she said.

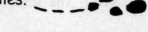

So that was the deal.

Told Revengers good news about concert at bus stop outside hospital. Now all I had to do was learn Chopin from scratch to concert standard in twenty-four hours. Aaron and Ralph had come up with a plan that involved intrigue, deception, kidnap and chocolate. I was dying to hear it. But before they could tell me another be-whiskered bus driver forced us to get on her bus.

'Has anyone got any money?' I asked.

We were chucked off the bus ten minutes later, but not before Aaron and Ralph had told me their plan. Dimitri Papayoti could play Chopin. So kidnap Dimitri and record him playing it. Then play the recording back at the concert so the audience would think it was *me*!

'And Giselle will realize that she has falsely accused me of being a liar and will therefore jump at the chance of making me happy by coming to our party on Sunday,' I said.

'Something like that,' said Ralph. 'How far is it to the Papayotis'?'

It was about six miles.

We kidnapped Dimitri from his front garden. Panos was supposed to be looking after him, but Panos forgets what day of the week it is when chocolate's mentioned, so we told him that the newsagent on the corner had just received a batch of Limited Edition Aeros. In a typical exhibition of big brotherly-ness he ran off and forgot all about his little brother. I knew he would. They always do.

Dimitri was nervous, especially when Napoleon wouldn't let us through the back door into the kitchen. He stood there with his pussy-hackles raised, hissing at us like a guard dog. I had to chuck him some raw steak out of the fridge to distract him.

'Stop worrying,' I told Dimitri, as we leaped over the slavering cat. 'No-one's going to eat you! I just want you to record Chopin for me.'

'What, *all* of it?' he said.

'No, just one piece,' I said. 'Mazurka in C.'

'If Daddy knew I was helping the enemy,' said Dimitri, 'he'd be really cross. He wants to beat you up.'

'The *enemy*?' I said. 'I'm your friend.'

'Remind me,' he said, 'do friends kidnap each other?'

I hate clever kids. They have a way of looking at you with their eyes that makes you feel as thick as six-ply cardboard.

In my bedroom Ralph set up the tape recorder while Dimitri poked Mr E on the window ledge. Since the accidents Mr E likes sitting next to open windows where the cool winds blow, because the plaster casts make him hot and pant with awful breath. Suddenly Dimitri screamed. 'It's alive! It opened an eye!'

'Of course it did. It's a dog,' I told him.

'I thought it was a really ugly ornament,' said Dimitri.

We were wasting time, so we sat Dimitri down and made him play, which he did brilliantly. But just as he finished there was a knock at the door and Giselle called out, 'Was that you playing, Alistair?'

It all happened so fast. I was just trying to get onto the piano stool before she came in. 'Off! Off!' I shouted, pushing Dimitri out of the way, but I must have pushed too hard, because suddenly Dimitri was flying through the open window, Mr E had vanished and William was helping

Dimitri out of the flowerbed. I heard the door click, sat down on the stool and rested my fingers on the keyboard.

'So it *was* you playing,' said Giselle. 'I thought you were lying when you said you liked Chopin.'

'I wouldn't lie to you,' I said.

'I know and I am sorry for thinking that. I look forward to the concert now,' she said, smiling for the first time in a while. 'It sounded very good.'

I could feel the Revengers willing me to ask her to come on Sunday, but my tongue was tied in knots again. We froze in awkward silence for at least a minute until Giselle's smiling muscles started hurting.

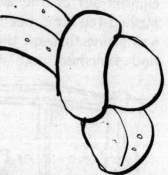

When she'd gone, Aaron and Ralph laughed nervously. 'She believed you,' said Aaron. 'She really thought that was *you* playing.'

'She doesn't know we were conning her,' said Ralph.

'Let's hope she never does,' I said, 'or she'll never come to our snogging party.'

I am going to Hell for all these lies.

I was in the street saying goodbye to the Revengers when Aaron spotted Mel and Colin coming back from the pub. We hid and watched. Mel sneaked round the back of the house, while Colin climbed up a ladder, waited at the top then climbed back down again, shouting, 'Finished!' so everyone could hear him.

17.25 – Have just realized the importance of this deadly information I have on Mel and Colin. I can use it to blackmail Mel into doing anything I want! So the big question is – what do I want? Big crash downstairs. Must go see what it is.

It was Mel. She was standing in the kitchen door with a smashed cup and plate at her feet. In the kitchen Cornelius was on the phone confirming tomorrow's delivery of a rubber shark, Giselle was sitting at the table eating a biscuit and Colin was making Giselle a cup of tea! Mel turned and looked at me furiously.

'What's the matter?' I said innocently. 'It's nice for Giselle to have a boyfriend, isn't it?'

Mel pushed me out of the way and burst into tears. Then she ran up the stairs, muttering to herself like a mad thing. 'Oh, Colin, how could you? Right. Rosie, here I come!'

It's getting better and better, but the big question still remains – what do I want?

I know what I *don't* want. I don't want to be told that Dimitri has broken his arm from falling out the window. I don't want to be told that he won't be playing in the concert. I don't want to be told that Mr Papayoti's on the warpath looking for the person responsible. And I don't want to be told all this by my big brother William. But I just have been.

The Cloud of Impending Doom

'At the moment, Mr Papayoti doesn't know you did it,' he said. 'I gave Dimitri a load of sweets to say he fell off a wall. So unless Dimitri or I tell him that you broke his arm *deliberately* to be the best pianist at Mrs Muttley's concert, you're safe. Which means,' he said slyly, 'that you're going to be extra super-nice to me, Alice. Understood?'

'What do you want me to do?' I said.

'I'll let you know,' he said.

It's the waiting I can't bear.

Mum cried at supper, because the kitchen was still a tip and the builders were way behind schedule. Whenever Colin's name was mentioned Mel wouldn't look me in the eye. Meal ended with Mum telling Dad to put a rocket up Mr Stratford. Giselle couldn't understand why putting an ugly pug dog up a builder should make him work faster.

usually alongside words such as lazy, workshy and layabout

← puzzled

scared ↓

ugly

Looked up pug dog in French = roquet.

129

22.50 – There has just been shouting from downstairs. Dad was on phone reading the riot act to Mr Stratford. I went down to sneak a peep. Dad trying to be angry is the second funniest thing in the world after Dad trying to do DIY. 'I want this job finished double time, Stratford, or there'll be *no* money. I don't care how many men it takes, just get them down here tomorrow morning, get that floor laid, get those walls tiled and get it done! Yes. Yes, thank you, the roof's working fine. Yes, no more leaks. It's lovely. Yes. And you. Nice to talk to you too. Take care. Bye. Love to your family and pets. Bye bye.' He slammed the phone down and, with his little face all glowing pink, turned to Mum. 'There,' he growled. 'Satisfied? Now who says I'm not a *real man*!' Then he fainted.

The doctor said it was due to blood loss on account of too many DIY accidents. 'Eat some steak,' said the doctor.

'I was planning to,' said Dad, 'but it mysteriously disappeared from the fridge.'

Why is everything that goes wrong on this planet *my* fault?

THINGS I DID NOT DO TODAY
1) Ask Giselle to party
2) Ask Giselle to party
3) Ask Giselle to party
4) Ask Giselle to party

I feel like a failure. Expect I am going to be a bag-lady when I grow up and make my shoes from car tyres. Tomorrow I MUST ask her, but how?

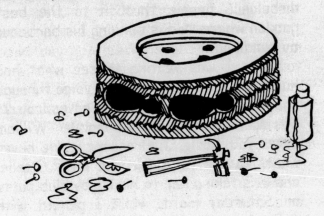

23.12 – Cunning flattery! Have just worked out a flattering French sentence for Giselle. It means, 'Giselle. You are as beautiful as a twinkling star.' And in French it sounds like this: *'Giselle, tu es aussi belle qu'un chien fou.'*

Sheer poetry.

23.16 – Mr E! Have just remembered. I forgot to look for Mr E when he fell into front garden. Checked out of window hoping to see white plaster casts glowing in the dark, but nothing. The good news is that the foxes won't be able to eat *all* of him, because most of him's covered in plaster armour.

23.45 – Heard ambulance siren pull up outside the house. Saw Mum leading the ambulance people through to the back garden where Dad is building his barbecue by candlelight.

While I was waiting to see what had happened, I heard a muffled voice through the wall. Used water glass to eavesdrop. It was Mel shouting on her mobile: 'William hates you, Rosie. Just accept it. He never wants to see you again. He loves Giselle, and he's taking her to his rugby club party on Saturday night, while I go out with Colin. So push off! You're dumped! OK?'

Does William know that Mel has just made that call?

23.48 – Dad was helped out of the back garden, pushed into the ambulance, then driven off at speed. I wonder which bit of him is missing now?

SATURDAY

The top of his ear. He caught it with the claw of his hammer on one of his back-swings, apparently. He showed me the chunk in the bathroom.

THINGS TO DO TODAY
1) Do not set myself too many impossible tasks
2) Ask Giselle to party

07.00 – The kitchen was like Piccadilly Circus. Twelve more builders turned up with Mr Stratford and Colin. Dad kept looking at Mum like he was Macho-Man of the Year for frightening Mr Stratford into bringing extra men this morning. 'And look,' he said, 'they're not drinking tea either. They're going straight out to work!' It was amazing.

Through the back door they went, up the scaffolding and into a huddle outside the guestroom window. It soon became clear that the extra men were only there because Colin had told them about Giselle. They wanted to spy on her through the window. Mel caught Colin offering Giselle a cup of tea from his thermos flask, and when she opened the window to accept it all the men cheered. Giselle laughed and Colin grinned and Mel slapped me round the head.

'What was that for?' I complained.

'For existing,' she said. I didn't argue. She had that look of Godzilla about her.

Giselle was happier today. She liked watching the builders. 'They are funny men,' she said, as

Melzilla

they wolf-whistled off the scaffolding. I nodded, but I wasn't listening. I was desperately trying to think of a way to steer the conversation onto parties.

Suddenly one of the builders cried out. He'd found a dog-shaped brick in the cement mixer. Fortunately it barked before he chucked it in the skip or we might never have seen Mr E again.

Mum rushed Mr E back to the Blue Cross Hospital. Dad would have taken him, but he'd accidentally nailed himself to his barbecue through his trouser pocket.

'Pets!' I said to Giselle. 'I don't know! I mean, don't you sometimes think that pets are just . . . well . . . like . . . parties?'

'No,' she said. 'Why?'

'Well, you *like* parties, don't you?' I said. 'And you *like* pets.'

'Not yours,'

she said. 'They are scary monsters.'

'But you *do* like parties?'

'That depends on who I am with!' she said.

And with that I couldn't say another word. If I asked her out now and she said no, I'd know I wasn't the type of person she wanted to go to a party with! I'd be destroyed. My confidence would plunge. It

a big plunge

my confidence

would wreck the rest of my life!

Rang the Revengers and told them I couldn't do it. They were heartbroken.

'But I've bought the crisps!' said Ralph.

'Just open your mouth and ask her,' said Aaron. 'It's not that hard.'

> It feels dead grown-up using that word.

'If you don't mind me saying so,' I said, 'that is a typical comment from a virgin.'

'Soldier!' said Ralph. 'In tonsil hockey war, failure is not an option! Now get back in there!'

But before I could move, a finger pressed the dial-tone button on the telephone and cut me off.

'Right,' said Mel. 'This is how it is. I will tell Mum and Dad about you and the hole in the roof unless *you* make sure that William takes Giselle to his rugby party tomorrow, so that I can have Colin all to myself. We made a date for tomorrow night that I am not missing!' She thought she had me cooked on toast, but I wasn't even crispy!

I have put this scene on freeze-frame while I discuss philosophy.

This was the moment in my life when I saw the value of knowledge. Having knowledge about Mel pulling Colin gave me choices. If I told people what I knew I could metaphorically manacle her to the wall and tip red ants over her hair. Or I could show her mercy and let her get away with her canoodling so long as I got what I wanted out of the deal. Let this be a lesson to all little brothers who come after me.

Getting knowledge is good. Blackmail is power. Here endeth the lesson. Amen. Back to the scene.

'No,' I said to Mel. 'The boot has turned. The worm is on the other foot. I will tell Mum and Dad what I know about you and Colin unless *you* ask Giselle to come to *our* party on Sunday night.'

'Me and Colin?' she said, like she didn't know what I was talking about.

'In the pub,' I said. 'I've got witnesses.'

Mel bit her lip, then struck back. 'I didn't think you were old enough to have a party, Alice.'

'Of course I am,' I said. 'It's a secret kissing party at Aaron's.' I realized too late what I'd done.

'Oh dear,' she said. 'You silly boy. You really must learn not to tell me all your secrets!' Ever been rolled over and stuffed like a Christmas turkey? 'Does Giselle know that you are lining her up for a snog-a-thon?'

'You wouldn't tell her,' I said.

'I would,' she said.

'If you do,' I said, 'I'll tell William how you told Rosie to get lost and never come back.'

'How do you know that?' she gasped.

'The night has ears,' I said mysteriously. 'And William will beat you up for causing him grief, because when Rosie's jealous she chucks red paint.'

'Who's Rosie?' said a voice at the top of the stairs.

Neither of us had seen Giselle coming. Mel looked embarrassed and ran into her room. I tried to lie, but couldn't think of anything other than the truth. 'Rosie's William's girlfriend,' I said.

Giselle smiled. 'Then I will come to *your* party, Alistair,' she said. 'But we see about snog-a-thon. I only kiss boys who I like.'

'Giselle,' I said, feeling a surge of hot blood in my veins, '*tu es aussi belle qu'un chien fou.*'

'Thank you,' she said. 'I am as beautiful as a mad dog. Nobody has ever said that to me before!' Then she touched my hand and disappeared into her room.

* Ralph was going to stop his dad becoming an alcoholic by nicking the lager from his dad's secret stash in the cellar.

'So can we nick the lager now?'* asked Ralph, when I told him that she'd said yes.

'How many cans?' said Aaron.

'How many people are coming?' I said.

'Six,' said Ralph. 'You, me, Aaron, my sister, Aaron's cousin and Giselle.'

'Well, bearing in mind that this is a proper party,' I said, 'and we *will* be letting our hair down . . . three cans! One between two. We are going to have the best time ever, I just know it!'

'I wonder if Giselle likes to kiss with the lights on or off?' said Ralph.

'Which do you prefer?' asked Aaron.

'Lights off,' he said. 'Then she can't see when I make a mistake.'

Mmm...Kiss Kiss

er...allo?..
Alistair?... I
eez over here!

The rest of the day leading up to the concert zipped by. It didn't stop raining, of course, but with so many workmen the roof was mended and the house was finished on time. It was too late to move the scaffolding, but Mr Stratford hid it behind a blue tarpaulin on top of which Cornelius painted the crest of a giant Australian wave. I painted teeth onto the rubber shark's mouth, the muddy grass was covered in sand, the eucalyptus was planted, the surfboards were scattered tastefully, Dad's authentic bush barbecue was finished and even Mum looked happy for the first time in a week. Up to here the day was good.

Then Mum paid Mr Stratford. Dad walked in on pound notes changing hands and suffered a loss of blood to his wallet. He fainted again. Unfortunately he was carrying his precious barbecue at the time, bringing it in for Mum to admire. It hit the ground just before he did and smashed into several tens of pieces. When Dad came round he cried for a bit, then picked up the wood, went back into the garden and started the rebuild straight away.

The other bad bit of the day happened

when William came home dripping with red paint. He wanted to know who'd told Rosie that he was in love with Giselle.

'Alice,' said Mel. 'For some reason he suddenly thinks he's rather good at blackmail, but he's not. Oh and by the way, William, Giselle can't come to your party on Sunday. She's babysitting Alice instead. Annoying little toad.'

I heard all of this and tried to hide, but William caught me climbing out of the window and fed me to my sofa. 'This time,' he said, 'you've poked your nose in too far, little brother. Tonight at the concert, watch your back. Mr Papayoti knows where you are.'

He hadn't gone and told him, had he?

Just in case, phoned Revengers for protection.

'You mean bodyguards!' laughed Aaron. 'But Mr Papayoti is six times bigger than me.'

'Bring a baseball bat,' I said.

'I don't play baseball,' said Aaron. 'I think my mum's got a badminton racket.'

Which was a confidence-builder just before I went on in front of my public.

Not many family members came to the concert. Dad was too busy with his new barbecue and William and Mel said that looking at my face all night would make them sick.

Mum, Giselle and I walked to the concert under umbrellas. I wore a big coat so I could hide the tape recorder in a pocket. Halfway there, Giselle leaned over and whispered in my ear. 'Once,' she said, 'I thought you were a liar and could not play piano at all. But now I know it is not true, I am glad.'

Then a weird thing happened. As we turned the corner before the church hall, the rain briefly stopped. For about thirty seconds the sky cleared and the stars came out. '*Regarde*,' said Giselle, pointing to a twinkling light just beyond the clouds. '*Une étoile scintillante.*' Then she laughed like Julia Roberts.

Blooming heck, I thought. Does she want to marry me?

Tomorrow night's party is going to be so extreme! I have this feeling in my bones that I am going to get kissed for the very first time!

143

Met bodyguards outside the church hall. Ralph had brought a baseball bat. Aaron had brought a frisbee. 'It was all I could find,' he said, as Granny Constance marched round the corner.

Mum said it was nice of her to come at such short notice. Granny replied, in a voice loud enough for everyone to hear, that she wouldn't normally be seen dead at such an amateur event, but the tea and chocolate biscuits were free.

Inside, it was a *huge* audience – at least thirty. So wheeling Mrs Muttley onto the stage in her padded wheelchair was really embarrassing. Not half as e m b a r r a s s i n g, though, as standing behind her while she told everyone what was wrong with her and showed off the anti-wart rubber gloves that she'd be wearing for lessons in future. Giselle looked mildly stunned.

Concert started with younger pupils who cannot play a note. As usual the standard was abysmal and Granny chose not to keep her thoughts to herself. 'Why does that dreadful woman in the wheelchair allow six-year-olds to play if they're so un-talented?' she said. Then it was my turn. 'Aren't you going to take your coat off?' she shouted as I stood up.

Only if I can put it over your head, I thought.

'*Bonne chance*,' said Giselle. 'Make this the best moment in my trip.'

I got the tape recorder into the piano OK, by leaning under the raised lid and pretending I was doing a bit of tuning. And I switched the tape on OK. It was a bit tricky knowing when to start playing, though, and I missed the first few notes. But after I'd caught up, I got into the swing of the mime, and with much tossing of hair, closing of eyes and panting on the fast bits I fooled the audience into think-ing that I was playing. When Dimitri had finished, I stood up and took a bow. Giselle was smiling. I thought I'd cracked it.

But I hadn't switched the tape off, and the next thing everyone heard was this . . .

GISELLE: Was that you playing, Alistair?

Scrape of piano stool.

ME: Off! Off!

Scream. Thump. Door click.

GISELLE: So it *was* you playing. I thought you were lying when you said you liked Chopin.

ME: I wouldn't lie to you.

GISELLE: I know and I am sorry for thinking that. I look forward to the concert now. It sounded very good.

Long pause.

Nervous laughter.

AARON: She believed you. She really thought that was *you* playing.

RALPH: She doesn't know we were conning her.

ME: Let's hope she never does, or she'll never come to our snogging party.

There was silence in the church hall while Giselle turned red. Then she stood up and ran outside, passing Mr Papayoti as he ran in.

'Alistair Fury!' he shouted. 'This audience comes to hear my genius boy Dimitri play Chopin, not you. You have broken his arm to become famous.'

'No,' I said, showing him the tape recorder. 'That *was* your son playing. I was miming. Look.'

Mrs Muttley swooned in horror. Miming was for louts on *Top of the Pops*, not for her classically trained pupils. Her reputation was in tatters!

Mr Papayoti refused to listen to reason and jumped over the pews to get at me. I had no choice but to hit him with the wheelchair. It was just unfortunate that Mrs Muttley was still in it at the time. her

scream of pain when she landed on her bottom shattered two stained-glass windows.

I dodged outside to find my two trusty bodyguards licking ice creams.

'He gave us two ninety-nines in exchange for the bat,' protested Ralph. 'You'd have done the same.'

'What was wrong with Giselle?' asked Aaron.

'Humiliated,' I said.

'And the kissing party?' said Ralph. 'She's still coming to that, isn't she?'

This was not a question I could answer.

When I got home, Dad was still in the garden rebuilding his barbecue. There was a lot less blood than I'd expected. 'I'm wearing gardening gloves,' he said, taking them off to show me and catching his knuckles on the metal rasper.

'**F****y g***t p*******n t*t*f*****s p*x**ktu**ct!**'

Now, where'd I heard that before?

Giselle had locked herself in her room. I tried to say sorry, but she just called me a liar and said that Colin was the only person she liked in England.

148

Later, when I was in bed, a note appeared under the door.

> By blackmail
> Date – Not before Time
> Alice You have driven Colin into the arms of another woman. You have driven ~~Rosie away~~. For all that you have done to wreck our ~~happiness~~,
> we hereby promise to get even.
> Beware!
> M & W

I was so scared that I didn't dare go out of my room for the rest of the night, not even when I wanted a pee. I held on for two hours until I couldn't hold on any more. Then I did it out the window.

'Oi!' came a shout from below.

'Sorry, Dad,' I shouted back. 'Just emptying my hot-water bottle.'

SUNDAY

07.15 – Mum's big day. Bet she's on the loo now with the nervous bum soup! Come to think of it, it's my big day too. If I'm lucky, really lucky, I mean the luckiest I've ever been in my whole life, I might get my first proper kiss today! Assuming the girl in question doesn't still hate me, of course.

Of all days in the history of the world for it not to rain this would have been the one. So it rained. And rained. And then it rained some more.

'It looks nothing like Bondi Beach,' shrieked Cornelius, as his sand turned dark brown and lumpy. 'It looks more like an accident at the Pilsbury Dough Boy Factory!'

Then the koala handler mentioned that his koala wasn't allowed to get wet on account of his sensitive chest, so Cornelius had to give it his anorak. Then Mr E thought the sand was a giant litter tray, and left a little peaked present for Cornelius, which reduced the inferior designer to his first crying fit of the day.

Mel and William stayed in bed with broken hearts, while Giselle refused to open her door and speak English, which made it impossible to understand anything

she was shouting. The Revengers came round to help out as waiters and I was given the job of official photographer, taking a video of all the famous faces.

An hour before kick-off, while Aaron, Ralph and me were stacking copies of Mum's new book in the hall as give-aways for each of the guests, Cornelius finally snapped. Mum was putting the finishing touches to a live lobster dip by posting parsley through the bars of the cage and supergluing it to the lobster's back, when Cornelius found her. Apparently, the Two

Rolfs had decided to paint an aboriginal emu on the tarpaulin *over* Cornelius's big surf, and Cornelius thought that what they'd done was rubbish. 'I told them,' he sobbed, 'I said, you stick to bad impersonations of a bearded Australian cat-lover, leave the party design to an expert! And they laughed. They *laughed* in my face, Celia! They pointed to your husband's barbecue and said, "Expert! Expert! Call yourself an expert designer with that monstrosity as your centrepiece!" And they're right, of course! Your husband's bush barbie *is* a monstrosity! It's hideous! I hate it!'

Dad's barbecue did look like a blind man had assembled it. 'I wanted it to have that unfinished look,' he said, which was just as well seeing as how he hadn't finished it. Then he started filling it with paper, firelighters, twigs and coal.

'Shouldn't you put the coal on later?' said Mum. 'It'll just be damp when we come to light it.'

'It'll light,' said Dad, unscrewing the lid from a keg of paraffin.

Granny Constance turned up early to see if there was anything she could do to get in the way.

'How are you at being a firelighter?' I said.

'We'll have less of the humour,' she said, 'and more of a cup of tea.'

My instructions were to film the guests arriving, then follow them around and catch them mingling. Unfortunately everyone mingled in the kitchen, because of the rain, so it was a bit like trying to film in the rush hour on the tube. Ralph, Aaron and me took it upon ourselves to get people outside onto Bondi Beach. We said, 'Ladies and gentlemen, the Australian Funnel Web Spider, the most deadly spider known to man, will shortly be joining us in the kitchen. You may stay indoors and enjoy its company if you wish.'

you know, I'm not so scary, I wanted to be a web designer

The room was cleared in four seconds.

154

But outside was just as cramped, because there were only four umbrellas to stand under and the koala had to have one to himself. And because Napoleon wouldn't stop biting people's ankles and Mr E wouldn't stop tripping people up with his sticky-out legs, Mum called me over.

'I want those animals out of here!' she hissed. 'And you're the only one who knows how to climb onto the kitchen roof, Alistair. Now, don't take any risks, but carry them up there, stick them in the tree so they can't get down, then leave them. We'll fetch them after the party.'

So that's what I did.

I did as I was told. It was an *accident*. One leg. Three or four tiles – that's all. And it was only a *small* hole.

By the time I got back into the kitchen, there was a nasty surprise waiting for me. William and Mel had got up. Not only that, but they were standing next to a huge puddle of water on Mr Stratford's new floor.

'It was an *accident*,' I said as the fresh hole in the roof leaked on and they strode off to find Mum and Dad.

Mum and Dad were standing in the rain arguing over the barbecue. Dad was trying to light it with great glugs of paraffin.

'It's too wet,' said Mum. 'We'll use the oven.'

'No,' shouted Dad. 'It *will* light!'

'Mum,' said William, 'can we have a word?'

'About Alistair,' said Mel.

They were going to do it! Only a miracle would save me now!

Well, what do you know? I must be blessed. The barbecue blew up like a petrol tanker and hurled flames twelve metres into the sky. Mum was knocked backwards into William and Mel. 'Inside!' she screamed at her guests, as burning ash fell on their heads.

It was a bit like when Vesuvius erupted.

But inside the floor was knee-deep in water and floating cookbooks.

'Will someone get that p**f**ink builder!' shouted Mum.

Colin arrived just as the barbecue set fire to the garden shed. I sent him up onto the kitchen roof to plug the hole, while Cornelius bounced into the hall, grabbed

Dad does not realize how easily other people pick up his fruity words.

Like the big scene from Gone with the Wind which Granny made me watch.

Cornelius

an heroic quivering lump of Jelly

the phone, and screamed, 'Fire! Fire! We're all going to die!'

'You've got to dial first,' I said. 'Nine-nine-nine.'

Mel and William ran through the hall with buckets. 'This is all your fault,' said William. 'You're going to pay.'

'You're dead meat!' said Mel. 'Smashing our hopes and dreams when all we ever wanted was love.'

'Virgins!' I said, as they ran into the garden to fight the fire. Then I ran upstairs to check that Colin knew how to get out onto the roof. But when I looked out of William's window, Colin wasn't there.

I found him in the guestroom. The door was open, Giselle was packed, and the two of them were kissing by the window. Outside the fire flickered through the blue tarpaulin like a backdrop to their passion.

'Sorry,' I said, but I don't think they

heard me, because they didn't stop kissing.

I jumped out of the room and shut the door behind me. A most brilliant revenge had just revealed itself to my brain. If William and Mel were going to grass me up to Mum and Dad, then it was my duty to pay them back for ever and ever until the end of time!

I rushed back into William's room and climbed out of his window. Only this time I didn't crawl across the roof, I climbed the scaffolding, and when I reached the top I untied the ropes that were holding the tarpaulin up. Like a grand theatrical curtain, the tarpaulin slid to the ground and revealed to the world, framed in the guestroom window, Colin and Giselle kissing!

DO NOT TRY THIS AT HOME

Well, not to the world, but to William and Mel, which was all that mattered. Both of them were crushed. Payback paradise!

They stood in the rain and cried. Mel had lost Colin and William had lost Giselle! Cornelius joined my brother and sister in a big hug. 'I know!' he bawled. 'Let it all out! This is the worst day of *my* life too!'

And it hadn't stopped getting worse either, because that was when the fire brigade arrived. They pushed their way into the garden and were not best pleased to see Mr E up a tree again.

'Knock him out with the hose,' said the officer who'd climbed the tree twice already. But as they tugged the hose through the house it got caught on a scaffolding leg.

'Look out!' I shouted. 'The scaffolding's moving.'

It was too. The hose had pulled the leg out of line and the structure was wobbling. As I slid back down a pole, Colin grabbed me and yanked me through the window. Just in time too, because seconds later the scaffolding collapsed. It smashed through the new roof, destroyed the new kitchen, fused all the lights, punctured the water main and collapsed the back wall, leaving the downstairs loo exposed to the watching world.

'Oh,' said Granny Constance, who was sitting on the loo with big pants round her ankles. 'Did I do that?'

Fifteen minutes later, when everyone had gone, Mum and Dad were sitting in the rain next to a big pile of ashes that had once been a barbecue and shed. They looked miserable. Their large drinks were half full of rainwater. Mum was talking to herself: 'Plink. Plink. Plink. That is the sound of rainwater in a gin and tonic. It is also the sound of despair.'

Mr E was barking in the tree. He didn't like being up there. Napoleon sat quietly beside him. He didn't seem to mind. Dad went inside and came back with a steak for the cat and a fish for the dog. Napoleon was the first to jump, but Mr E lost his nerve.

'He can't jump from there,' I said. 'Not with his plastered legs.'

'Yes he can,' said Dad. 'He can suffer like the rest of us. Come on, boy, you can make it.'

He didn't. Mr E landed on my head and knocked me out.

Nobody jumped up to save me.

In the blackness I had a beautiful dream. Giselle ran towards me wearing gossamer wings and a floaty white nightie. As she leaned over me her hair tickled my cheeks and then she kissed me. A long, beautiful, slightly wet, slightly snuffly kiss!

And when I woke up, I was being kissed by Mr E again!

17.15 – I discovered this note from Giselle on my pillow. Her room was empty. Her bags had gone.

Dear Alistair,
You are only person I can tell this to, because you are not as mad as other mad people in your house. I have left your house. It is not the fact that your big sister hate me, or that William and your best friend want to kiss me, or that your granny think she is the queen, or that your dog is a cat and your cat is a vampire, or that your mama is a TV cook who can't cook, or even that your papa is one of the living dead, because he walk around all the time with no blood in him, it is that I really want to snog Colin and I know I can't do that in your house. Please do not try to find me. I have gone to a better place. Herne Hill.

                                    Giselle

19.00 – Mel refused to believe this letter. She has dolled herself up and is waiting in the hall for Colin to turn up for their date. She will be waiting all night. *I hope!*

Sulky William has just slouched off to his rugby party alone, which only goes to prove that trying to have your cake *and* eat it just leads to a great big mess of crumbs in your lap. A lesson for everyone

there, I think.

For me, the problem is telling the Revengers about the lack of Giselle.

The party was really happening when I

arrived. There was music playing and all the furniture was back against the walls. When I told them that Giselle wasn't coming, Ralph looked like he'd been shot and Aaron just shrugged.

'We can still have a good time,' he said.

'Yes,' said Ralph's sister, putting her arm round Aaron's cousin. 'We're still here, or don't we count as girls?'

'No,' said Ralph. 'You don't count. You're my sister.'

'*I'm* not,' said Aaron's cousin. 'You can talk to me.'

So we agreed that Ralph would talk to Aaron's cousin and Aaron would talk to Ralph's sister and I would talk to anyone who wasn't already talking to someone else.

We shared the three cans of lager. The crisps didn't last long, because we were all hungry. I remembered to offer one to Aaron's cousin, but Ralph got in first with the nuts.

'No thank you,' she said. As his bowl went back I thrust mine forward, but she didn't want a crisp either.

'But these are *thick*,' I said, 'with fifty per cent extra potato. They're the best.'

She still didn't want one.

Once the food had gone we got bored of sitting down and wondered what we could do next.

'We could dance,' said Ralph's sister.

Aaron and Ralph snorted. 'I can't dance,' said Aaron. But Aaron's cousin could do

ballet and said she'd teach us. So Ralph, Aaron and me had to follow Aaron's cousin in all sorts of ballet steps that were sometimes rude and always girly – like pointing our fingers and toes and making arms like a big tree. I bet Cornelius is good at ballet, but not me. Still, the falling over gave Ralph the opportunity to pretend to trip

She wouldn't have known, but it wasn't an accident at all - he told me later!

and fall into Aaron's cousin's lap. As he stood up, he tried to brush his cheek against her hand *by accident* but she pulled her hand away and said, 'Are you all right?' like a mum would do.

Aaron felt the pressure of being party host. Afterwards he told me that he had worried all evening that people weren't enjoying themselves enough. That was why he'd suggested a game of Postman's Knock or watching a James Bond video.

'Shame there's not a conjuror here,' said Ralph's younger sister.

'Shut up, fat face,' said Ralph. 'Nobody's interested in what you want.' He sounded just like William.

22.00 – We'd played Battleships and two rounds of charades, and Ralph had got a bit drunk drinking all the dregs of all the three cans, when Aaron's cousin stood up. 'Time to go home, I think,' she said.

At which point Ralph started crying. The party was pretty much over after that.

On the way home I walked past a party in a house with its door open. Loud music thumped out onto the street, mixed with shrieks and screams and laughter, and the ground rocked with hundreds of sweaty people jumping and dancing and having the time of their lives. Without exception I hated *everyone* in that building.

22.30 – Found Mel still dressed up, still sitting in the hall where I left her. Colin had never turned up. Mel had black streaks down her face where her make-up had run from the tears.

Ho ho!

23.05 – Just realized. Still haven't had a proper kiss. It'll be just my luck if I stay a virgin all my life!

MONDAY

School still closed due to flood warning.

Best news was at home, though. William and Mel have changed. Since they woke up this morning they have been nothing but sunshine. They've been helping to clear up, shovelling sand, washing plates and glasses, mopping the floor, and even talking to me like I was a normal person. I've actually started to *like* them!

I think they were trying to cheer up Mum and Dad. Mum felt that yesterday had not gone quite as well as she'd hoped. So Mel suggested that we watched the video I'd shot, because that would prove to Mum that people *had* loved the party, *had* loved the new book and *did* love Mum.

After supper William got the tape out of the camera and put it into the video. 'Everyone comfy?' he asked. Mum and Dad were ready on the sofa. 'Then let us begin!'

I should have known what was coming from the smirks on the faces of my big brother and sister, but I didn't spot them. William pressed PLAY and the TV screen kicked into life.

William, Mel and I were sitting in Mel's room. William and Mel had their backs to the camera and appeared to be sleeping. I had a book on my lap on how to hypnotize pets. In a distant, faraway voice, William was saying, 'Carry on, Great Guru.'

'Oh yes,' said Mel. 'Fill us with your wisdom.'

'Right,' I said. 'Get this! You have forgotten everything you saw on the roof where Alistair made that hole with his clumsy feet. It never happened . . .'

I leaped up and pressed the PAUSE button, but the cat was already out of the bag.

'What hole?' said Mum. 'Was it you who made the first hole in the roof, Alistair?'

THURSDAY

I hid for three days.

Actually I lived at Mrs Muttley's. I span her a lie. I said that my parents had sent me out of the house and told me not to come back until I had worked off my sinning behaviour at her concert. She was very pleased to take me in as a slave and made me her official rubber-ring pumper-upper and wart warden. Being a wart warden involved checking her warts with a magnifying glass every hour to see if they'd grown more crinkly.

'If they start to look like muffins, I'm in trouble!' she said.

I also got two hours of piano practice every day, which means that I can now play Chopin. I still hate him.

When I got back home, Dad was trapped underneath the garden shed after trying to rebuild it. You couldn't see him, but you could hear his voice:

F****y g***t
P**-******N ***
P**X**KTU**CT!!!

William and Mel were both out on dates with their new girlfriend and boyfriend, and Mum was cooking Broiled Dog in Wooftershire Sauce. At least, that's what it smelled like!

'Oh, there you are,' she said calmly. She didn't seem the slightest bit concerned that I'd been missing! 'Giselle called round to see you before she went back to France. She wanted to kiss you goodbye.'

'F**** y g***t p**-*****n t*t*f*****s p*x**ktu**ct!'

Le Vin

ABOUT THE AUTHOR

Jamie Rix originally started writing and producing comedy for TV and radio, including such programmes as *Alas Smith and Jones* starring Mel Smith and Griff Rhys Jones, and *Radio Active*. Jamie's first children's book, *Grizzly Tales for Gruesome Kids,* was published in 1990 and won the Smarties Prize Children's Choice Award. Since then he has written children's books for a wide variety of age groups, including *Johnny Casanova – the Unstoppable Sex Machine,* for older readers, and several sequels to the *Grizzly Tales...* This book and its sequels have been adapted into an award-winning television animation series.

Jamie's first book for Young Corgi was the very funny *One Hot Penguin,* which *The Times Educational Supplement* called 'an excellent book with a double-edged resolution'. His latest project is a series of books containing THE WAR DIARIES OF ALISTAIR FURY – the hilarious account of an eleven-year-old boy desperate for revenge on his older brother and sister.

Jamie is married with two grown-up sons and, like Alistair Fury, he lives in Tooting, London.

THE WAR DIARIES OF ALISTAIR FURY

Bugs on the Brain

Jamie Rix

BONSAI! THIS IS WAR

My big brother and sister, William and
Mel, may be older than me and biggerer
than me, but they're not cleverer than me.
Just because the chips of the world are stacked
against me like a potato mountain doesn't mean they can
beat me. Revenge will be mine!

Or rather mine and the Revengers', and a boa constric-
tor called Alfred's. Let loose the snakes of doom and
see how they like it then! I shall have my revenge
before you can say 'peanut butter and jam sandwiches'!
Actually I shouldn't have mentioned peanut butter and
jam sandwiches. Forget you ever read that. If you
don't, I may have to kill you.

*The first book in a brilliant and hilarious series by
award-winning comic writer, Jamie Rix.*

CORGI YEARLING BOOKS

THE WAR DIARIES OF ALISTAIR FURY

Dead Dad Dog

Jamie Rix

Mum, Dad, William and Mel are ill. It's 'Fetch this, Alistair; bring that, Alistair...' all day long. Huh! Do they think I'm their slave? I'm far too busy sorting out my own problems. First, there's Mrs Muttley and her persistent piano lessons. (I don't know why she won't believe that my fingers have fallen off.)Then there's the bright yellow trousers that my mum bought me – and the photo of me taken without any trousers on at all! To say nothing of Great-Uncle Crawford and the disappearing suit, or Miss Bird and the repulsive recipes...

The only kind ones in this family are the pets – and a vampire dog and an unstable cat aren't much use. Luckily I've still got my real friends – the Revengers – and a ghost of an idea of how to get my own back on the family.

The second book in a brilliant and hilarious series by award-winning comic writer, Jamie Rix.

CORGI YEARLING BOOKS

30

I'm almost ready for Christmas. Gran's booked tickets for the home match on Boxing Day, so that's the basics sorted. I've helped trim the house and put the tree up but I'm way behind on my Christmas cards. Writing. Ugh! That reminds me. Any old mates out there who want to get in touch can contact me at:

Danny Ogle
  Cool Cottage
    Nice Country Lane
      Loads to Do
        The Pleasant Countryside
          England

Life's great, isn't it?